THE BRIDES *of* BELLA ROSA

Romance, rivalry and a family reunited.

For years Lisa Firenzi and Luca Casali's sibling rivalry has disturbed the quiet, sleepy Italian town of Monta Correnti, and their two feuding restaurants have divided the market square.

Now, as the keys to the restaurants are handed down to Lisa's and Luca's children, will history repeat itself? Can the next generation undo their parents' mistakes, reunite their families and ultimately join the two restaurants?

Or are there more secrets to be revealed?

The doors to the restaurants are open, so take your seats and look out for secrets, scandals and surprises on the menu!

BARBARA HANNAY

Executive:

Expecting Tiny Twins

THE BRIDES
of
BELLA ROSA

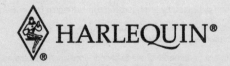

TORONTO • NEW YORK • LONDON
AMSTERDAM • PARIS • SYDNEY • HAMBURG
STOCKHOLM • ATHENS • TOKYO • MILAN • MADRID
PRAGUE • WARSAW • BUDAPEST • AUCKLAND

Recycling programs
for this product may
not exist in your area.

ISBN-13: 978-0-373-17656-4

EXECUTIVE: EXPECTING TINY TWINS

First North American Publication 2010.

Special thanks and acknowledgment are given to Barbara Hannay for her contribution to The Brides of Bella Rosa series.

Barbara Hannay was born in Sydney, educated in Brisbane and has spent most of her adult life living in tropical North Queensland, where she and her husband have raised four children. While she has enjoyed many happy times camping and canoeing in the bush, she also delights in an urban lifestyle— chamber music, contemporary dance, movies and dining out. An English teacher, she has always loved writing, and now, by having her stories published, she is living her most cherished fantasy.

Visit www.barbarahannay.com.

Next month, follow the story of Isabella's
rebellious cousin, Valentino Casali,
who's coming home to Monta Correnti!

Miracle for the Girl Next Door
by Rebecca Winters

CHAPTER ONE

SHE was wearing white, for crying out loud.

Jack Lewis grimaced as the elegant figure stepped down from the tiny plane while clouds of red dust slowly settled on the airstrip. The same red dust covered his ute, his riding boots, and practically everything else in the outback, and yet Senator Elizabeth Green had chosen to arrive on Savannah cattle station dressed from head to toe in blinding, laundry-commercial white.

Her elegant sandals were white, her crisply ironed trousers, her matching linen top and even her floppy-brimmed hat. The only non-white items were her accessories—swanky dark glasses and a pale green leather shoulder bag that clearly held a laptop.

Where did she think she'd flown to? The flaming Italian Riviera?

Jack muttered a soft oath, audible only to Cobber, the cattle dog at his heels. 'I suppose we'd better go and say g'day.'

Shrugging off an uncomfortable sense of martyrdom, Jack set out across the stretch of dirt, moving with a deliberately easy amble, his faithful dog close behind him.

He was mad with himself for allowing his boss, an

eighty-year-old widow, to bully him into hosting this visitor. Kate Burton regularly tested Jack's patience by directing her business via long-distance phone calls from her top-price-tag retirement home in Melbourne.

'I owe Lizzie a favour,' Kate had told him breezily. 'She won't be any trouble, Jack. She just wants to rest up and take in the country air, and she needs to retreat from the public eye for a spell. You understand, don't you?'

After a lifetime of getting her own way, Kate hadn't given Jack the chance to protest that no, he didn't understand, that he was managing her cattle station not a hotel, that the mustering season had started and he was planning to join the team.

For her part, Kate made no attempt to explain why a high-profile senator, the darling of the Canberra media, was suddenly diving for cover in distant North Queensland.

Kate had left Jack with no choice but to send out the mustering team while he remained behind at the homestead. This morning he'd dutifully rounded up the horses grazing in this paddock, and he'd flattened the anthills that had popped up on the airstrip since the last time a light plane had landed here.

Now, as he approached his guest, she straightened her shoulders and lifted her chin—her very neat and determined chin.

Her shady white hat and dark glasses hid the top half of her face, but Jack sensed her surprise, as if he wasn't quite what she'd expected.

He was having the same problem—madly readjusting his assumptions. Up close, Senator Elizabeth Green was a bombshell.

He'd seen photos of her in newspapers, of course, and he was aware of her classic Italian good looks, but he'd expected the real-life version to be closer to Iron Maiden than Sophia Loren. Surely this woman was too soft and sensuous to be a federal politician?

Jack could see curves beneath her crisp white linen clothes—old-fashioned, reach-out-and-touch-me curves.

Her dark hair was tucked up under her hat, but silky wisps had strayed onto her nape, drawing his attention to her super-smooth, pale skin with a dusky hint of the Mediterranean.

As for her mouth…

Whoa. Her mouth was wide and full and soft and sultry, quite possibly the sexiest mouth Jack had ever met.

Her mouth moved. 'Mr Lewis?'

It took Jack a second or two to get his brain on the right track.

'Good morning, Senator.' He spoke a little too loudly. 'Welcome to Savannah.'

He wondered if she was going to offer her hand. Her big hat and sunglasses hid so much of her that he found it hard to pick up clues, but he sensed she was still checking him out, trying to make as many correct assumptions as possible.

When at last she offered her hand, it was cool and slim, her grip firm.

'I have luggage.' Despite the faint Italian accent, when the senator spoke she was Iron Maiden through and through.

Reassured that he knew what he was dealing with, Jack waved to the pilot. 'I'll get the luggage, Jim.'

In the hold, he found two large and perfectly matched green leather suitcases—*Louis Vuitton, of course*—and a matching leather holdall filled with books. When he hefted the strap over his shoulder, the books weighed a ton.

'I see you plan to do a little light reading,' he said, offering her a grin.

The senator gave a slight shrug, as if it was obvious that she'd have little else to do out here except improve her mind.

Reducing his grin to a resigned smile, Jack waved to the pilot, then picked up the suitcases. Hell, judging by the weight of them, she planned to move in to Savannah for six months. Or longer. Kate Burton had been vague about the length of this visitor's stay.

'We'd better get going before Jim takes off and creates another dust storm.' Jack nodded in the direction of his parked ute. 'The limousine's this way.'

Again, Senator Green didn't acknowledge Jack's attempt at a joke. Instead, she looked over at the vehicle covered in dust and then gazed slowly about her, taking in the wide and empty red plains dotted sparsely with clumps of grey-green grass, and at the sky, huge, blue and cloudless. Boundless.

A lone crow's cry pierced the stillness. *Ark, ark, ark!*

Watching his guest closely, Jack saw her take a breath as if she were bracing herself for an ordeal. He had no interest in her problems or why she'd come here, yet to his dismay he felt a faint pang of sympathy.

They set off for the ute and by the time they reached it— a matter of sixty metres or so—Senator Green's sandals were filmed with red dust and a faint red rim showed at the bottom of her pristine trousers.

Her mouth pursed with sour-lemon tightness as she watched Jack set her glamorous luggage next to bales of fencing wire in the tray back of his battered ute.

'Hope you weren't expecting anything too flash.' He opened the passenger door, saw dog hairs on the seat, and, despite an urge to leave them there, swept the seat clean with the brim of his Akubra hat.

'Thank you,' the senator said in a princess-speaking-to-the-footmen tone.

Jack wished he hadn't bothered.

'How far is it to the homestead?' she asked.

'Not far. A couple of kilometres.'

She nodded, but chose not to comment.

'In the back, Cobber,' Jack ordered, and his dog obediently jumped up beside the pale green luggage. 'And you'd better fasten your seat belt,' he told his passenger as he swung into the driver's seat. 'It's bound to be a bumpy ride.'

Lizzie sat in grim silence as the ute set off across the trackless ground. She was grateful that Jack didn't try to carry on a conversation, yelling above the roar of the motor. He seemed happy enough to drive while she clung to the panic handle, which she needed more to steady her nerves than because the ride was rough.

She needed to calm down, to throw off the alarming schoolgirl thrill that had flared inside her the instant she'd set eyes on Jack Lewis.

Good grief. It was ridiculous. Laughable. She hadn't felt such an instantaneous, unwarranted reaction to a man for almost a decade. She'd thought she'd developed immunity.

For heaven's sake. It was absurd and distressing to feel this fireworks-in-her-very-veins excitement at the sedate age of forty. It was a joke. She would put her reaction down to surprise. She'd expected Jack Lewis to be older, several decades older, actually.

After her conversation with Kate Burton, she'd had an image of the manager of Savannah as a mature and kindly, grey-haired man of the land. He'd be a little shy perhaps, as rural folk were reputed to be. Reliable, dependable, salt of the earth. A fatherly figure, possibly a bit like her dad.

Lizzie couldn't have been further from the mark.

Jack was young, younger than she was, for sure, and he had all the attributes of a hunky pin-up boy—height, fitness, muscles, glowing health. Throw in sun-bleached hair and sparkling green eyes and a smile that would melt granite, and the man was borderline dangerous.

The silly thing was, Lizzie had met oodles of good-looking men without going weak at the knees, but there was something else about this fellow, something elusive.

Perhaps it was the slow and easy way he moved. She thought about the way he'd approached her with a leisurely, loose-hipped stride, and the effortless way he'd hefted her luggage as though it held nothing but tissue paper. Even the way he drove was relaxed and easy—guiding the steering wheel with one hand, while his other hand rested lightly on the gear stick.

Sex appeal in spades.

No doubt the young women for miles around were all in love with him.

Good grief. She had to stop thinking like this. *Now!*

Jack Lewis wasn't her type. Not remotely. She was a federal senator, earnest and conscientious—busy, busy, busy. Everything about Jack—his lazy smile and his easy, laid-back body language—showed that his whole attitude to life was different from hers.

Of course, Lizzie knew she shouldn't react to superficial appearances. She'd learned early in her career that if she genuinely wanted to find ways to help people, she had to look below the surface. Things were rarely as they appeared. The truth was always hidden.

As a woman, she also knew that she had a bad habit of

falling for the wrong man. Twice in her life, she'd met someone she'd found instantly attractive. Twice she'd been burned, almost reduced to ashes.

Never again. With good reason—two very handsome reasons—she'd made a conscious decision to keep her private life a male-free zone. Men. Just. Weren't. Worth. It.

She'd been relieved to finally step off the dating-relationship merry-go-round, and she couldn't believe she'd wasted so many years trying to choose a life partner. Now she embraced the freedom of going it alone, just as her mother had. In fact, she was taking her independence one step further than her mother had.

The ute bounced and rattled over a cattle grid and Lizzie automatically placed a protective hand over the tiny bulge below her navel.

Her baby.

Hers and only hers.

The past three months had flown so quickly, and, according to the pregnancy books that Lizzie had studied in depth and learned by heart, her baby was already the size of half a banana. It would have tiny fingerprints now, and if it was a little girl, she would have about two million eggs in her ovaries.

'Are you OK?' Jack sent Lizzie a quick look of concern that took in the protective hand on her stomach.

'I'm fine, thank you.' She spoke brusquely. Tension made her brittle and she quickly lifted her hand and fiddled with a stray wisp of hair, tucking it under her hat.

The last thing she wanted was to draw attention to her growing baby bump. Kate Burton had promised not to mention her pregnancy to Jack, and Lizzie certainly didn't want to explain until she got to know him better.

Come to think of it, Lizzie couldn't imagine taking Jack

into her confidence. Surely there would be someone else at the homestead, perhaps a kindly housekeeper, who would be happy to indulge in heart-to-heart chats over a cup of tea. She should have asked Kate Burton more questions.

Looking out at the endless stretch of red plains, Lizzie felt her spirits swoop. She was planning to spend at least a month out here in the back of beyond. She needed the break, for the baby's sake, and for sanity's sake, and she surely needed to escape from the hound dogs in the press gallery.

If they caught a sniff of Jack, I'd be in trouble.

The isolation should keep her safe, however, and somehow she would cope.

She planned to keep busy, of course, staying in touch with her office in Brisbane and her parliamentary colleagues in Canberra via her laptop and her mobile phone— her *new* mobile phone, with a number that she'd only shared with a discreet circle of people she could trust.

In her spare time she would work her way through the supplementary reading matter she'd brought with her. She'd always complained that she never had enough time for reading for pleasure, although once upon a time she'd liked nothing better than losing herself in a good book.

She'd also imagined going for pleasant country walks, except this flat, parched land didn't look very inviting.

'Here's the homestead,' Jack said, pulling up at a gate and pointing ahead through the dusty windscreen.

It was a timber building, long and low, and painted white. It had a dark green, corrugated iron roof, and there were several smaller buildings scattered around it. Sprawled beneath the harsh outback sun, the collection of buildings made Lizzie think of a sleepy dog with a litter of puppies.

Jack sent her a sideways glance loaded with expectation,

and she realised she was expected to say something. But what?

There was no garden to admire, although the curving lines of stones cemented together suggested that there might have been gardens in the past. She supposed she would be comfortable enough here, but the house looked very lonely sitting in the middle of the flat empty plains.

She said, 'The house looks…very…nice.'

There was a glimmer of impatience in his glance. *What is his problem?*

'Do you think you could get the gate?' he asked, super-politely.

The gate?

'Oh-h-h…the gate.' Lizzie gave a shaky laugh to cover her shock. In Canberra, she had a swipe card that opened doors or gates in a split second, or her staff went ahead of her, smoothing the way. 'You'd like *me* to open it?'

He gave her a wry smile. 'It's sort of bush tradition. Driver stays at the wheel. Passenger opens the gate. So, if it's not too much trouble.'

This gate proved to be a great deal of trouble.

First Lizzie had to wrestle with the door handle, then she had to clamber down from the ute into several inches of fine red dust that once again covered her sandals and seeped between her bare toes. Finally, she spent an embarrassing age at the gatepost, wrestling with a heavy metal loop and a complicated piece of rusty wire.

Pride wouldn't allow her to give in, but she hadn't a clue how to get the thing open.

A deep and very annoying chuckle brought her whirling around. Jack Lewis had left the truck and was standing close behind her, grinning. 'I guess I'd better show you how it works.'

'I guess you'd better,' she snapped. 'This is the most ridiculous gate I've ever seen. What's the point of making it so difficult? Why can't you have a normal latch?'

'That'd be too easy. Even the cattle could work out how to open it.'

Her response was a disdainful sniff, and she watched him with tightly closed lips as he tilted the metal loop, and, with the swift ease of a conjuring trick, slipped the wire hook free, letting the gate swing easily open.

He winked at her. 'Did you get that?'

'Of course,' she said stiffly, unwilling to admit that she wasn't completely sure how he'd done it.

'Good-o. I'll take the ute through, and you can close it after me.'

'Wait!' Lizzie commanded as he headed back to the truck.

Jack turned super-slowly, an ambiguous smile lurking in his eyes.

Her shoulders stiffened and her chin hiked higher. 'You didn't show me how to close it.'

With a lazy shake of his head he ambled back to her, and she couldn't tell if he was smiling at her expense, or trying to be friendly.

Unfortunately, he stood too close as he refastened the gate, and Lizzie found herself distracted by the play of muscles in his tanned forearms and the deft movements of his brown fingers.

'You tilt it at two o'clock,' he said, showing her twice. 'Here, you have a go.'

Their hands brushed, making her skin flash with ridiculous heat, but at last she had the hang of it, and, of course, it was dead easy once she knew.

Back in the truck, they trundled on till they reached the front steps, and Jack retrieved Lizzie's luggage with the same easy economy of movement that she found so unsettling. This time she tried very hard not to watch.

At the top of the steps he turned to her. 'I guess you'd like to see your room first.'

'Thank you.'

'It opens off this veranda.'

His blue cattle dog curled in a pool of sunlight on the veranda, while Lizzie followed its master, carrying her laptop, and shamelessly watching the man from behind, noting the way his broad shoulders stretched the seams of his blue cotton shirt, and his faded jeans rode low on his lean hips.

Good grief, Lizzie. Give it a miss.

Jack turned through French doors into a large, airy room and set Lizzie's bags on the beige carpeted floor beside the big bed with old-fashioned brass ends and a soft floral spread. He watched Lizzie look about her, inspecting the pale pink walls and fine, white spotted curtains.

'This is the room Kate uses when she visits Savannah,' he told her.

Lizzie nodded. 'I could well believe that. It's just like Kate—comfortable, relaxing and no-nonsense.'

And you're damn lucky to have it, he thought. *It's the best room in the house.*

Lizzie looked at the painting above the bed, a watercolour of a flock of birds taking off against a soft pink dawn.

'Kate thought you'd like it in here,' he said.

'It's very kind of her to let me use her room. I do like it. Very much.'

OK. One hurdle over, Jack thought.

But then two vertical lines creased Lizzie's forehead. 'Is there an en suite?'

He shook his head, and took perverse glee in saying, 'The bathroom's down the hall.'

'Oh, right.' Lizzie lifted her limp shirt collar away from her neck. 'I don't suppose there's air-conditioning?'

'The ceiling fans are adequate. It's not summer. You'll be OK.' He pointed to the large, silky oak table next to the window with a view across the paddocks. 'Kate said you needed a desk, so I put this here for you.'

'Thank you.' Lizzie sent a final queenly glance around the room, then slipped her laptop bag from her shoulder and set it on the desk, giving the laptop an affectionate pat, as if it was her best friend—or her lifeline.

Then she removed her sunglasses and set them beside the laptop, and took off her big white hat, which should not, of course, have been a big deal.

But *hell.*

Jack's body reacted as if Lizzie had launched into a striptease.

She'd accidentally dislodged her hairpins, and her hair—thick, lustrous, shiny and as dark as midnight—spilled to her shoulders, and suddenly he was having difficulty breathing.

Which was probably just as well. If he'd been able to draw breath, he might have spoken, might have said something crazy, like telling her she was out-of-this-world beautiful.

Because—damn it, she was. She was stunning. Her eyes were the most amazing hazel, with flecks of earthy brown and mossy green stippled with gold. As for her face, framed by all that silky dark hair—

Jack could feel the muscles in his throat working overtime as he stood there like a fool, staring. At her.

Until she frowned, then looked worried. Nervous.

Somehow, he dragged in a necessary breath, and switched his gaze to the desk, forced his mind back to business. 'I—I believe you—you've brought your own Internet connection?'

'Yes.' Lizzie also took a breath, and she lifted her shirt collar again, pulling it away from her flushed skin. 'I—um—have a wireless broadband mobile card.'

'Sounds brilliant.'

'It's handy for travelling.'

She took another breath, deep and slow, then began to twist her hair back into a safe, neat, spinsterish knot.

Jack rammed his hands hard into the pockets of his jeans and looked about him—anywhere but at her. 'So what would you like to do? Unpack and settle in here? Or take a gander at the rest of the house?'

Lizzie hesitated, dismayed that her mind was so fuddled she found the simplest decision difficult. Given the amount of work she had to do, she should unpack her laptop and get started immediately.

'Perhaps you need a cuppa first,' Jack suggested slowly, almost reluctantly.

There would be a housekeeper in the kitchen. Someone sensible and cosy to provide a reassuring buffer between Lizzie and this disturbingly attractive, but highly unsuitable man. She found herself saying, 'Tea would be lovely, thanks.'

Once again, she followed Jack, this time down a narrow hallway and through a large living room filled with deep squishy lounge chairs and low occasional tables, with two sets of French doors opening onto a veranda. Casting a quick glance around the room, she gained an impression of casual relaxation and carelessness.

Cushions had been left in a tumbled pile at one end of the sofa, clearly for the comfort of the person who'd lain there watching television. Sporting magazines and empty coffee cups were strewn about, and an overturned beer can lay on the floor beside the sofa. The housekeeper was obviously as casual as Jack.

Lizzie thought fondly of her minimalist, twenty-first-century apartment and her super-efficient cleaning woman, and sighed.

They reached the kitchen.

'Pull up a pew.' Jack nodded to one of the mismatched chairs gathered around a huge, scrubbed pine table that had one end cleared, while the rest was littered with magazines, newspapers, an assortment of mail, a hammer, nails and a leather strap with buckles that might have been part of a horse's bridle.

To Lizzie's surprise, he went to the sink and filled a kettle, turned on the gas and set it on the stove.

Where was the friendly, pink-cheeked, country housekeeper, waiting with a warming teapot and a batch of scones just out of the oven?

'Is it the housekeeper's day off, Jack?'

He frowned. 'What do you mean?' His eyes narrowed as he sent a puzzled look around the shabbily out-of-date kitchen. 'Is there something wrong?'

With growing dismay, Lizzie watched him reach up to a shelf above the stove for a caddy of loose-leaf tea. He did it automatically, with the familiar ease of someone who'd done this a thousand times. 'You do have a housekeeper, don't you?'

Jack shook his head. 'No need. There's just me in the main house.' He sent her a wry quarter-smile. 'Kate said you wanted a retreat. She didn't say anything about luxury.'

'I'm not asking for luxury.'

Jack's eyebrow rose, but he spoke quietly, 'That's all right, then.'

He poured a little hot water into the teapot, swirled it around and then tipped it into the sink before he added tea leaves. Once again, Lizzie watched his hands—

strong, long and capable, with golden, sun-bleached hairs on the backs.

Damn. She shouldn't have been watching Jack Lewis's hands. She was over men. Twice bitten, permanently shy. Besides, Jack was much younger than she was—and she'd come here to escape, to retreat in peace and quiet: optimum conditions for a healthy pregnancy. Already, she felt agitated and edgy. It was Jack's fault. No, it was hers. She simply had to control her reactions.

Of course, if she told Jack she was pregnant, she would clear the air instantly. Such news would quickly kill that sexy sparkle in his eyes, and she might be able to let her hair down without the world coming to a standstill.

She could get on with her plan to relax at Savannah while her baby grew healthy and strong.

She opened her mouth, already tasting the words: *By the way, Jack, I'm pregnant.*

But suddenly she knew she wasn't going to tell him. She'd come to this outpost to avoid giving explanations about her pregnancy to a pack of hungry journalists. There was no need to tell Jack. Not yet.

Maybe later.

Maybe never. He was a stranger, after all, and Lizzie's pregnancy was none of his business.

Very soon, her hormones would settle down and this inappropriate sense of attraction would die a natural death.

CHAPTER TWO

'DO YOU do all your own cooking?' Lizzie asked Jack, forcing her mind to practical matters.

'Not usually. Most of the time there's a station cook, but I sent him out with the mustering team.' Jack poured boiling water into the teapot, replaced the lid and set the pot on the table with two blue striped mugs.

'Is there a muster on at the moment?'

He nodded. 'We always muster as soon as the wet season's out of the way.'

'Does that mean I've inconvenienced you?'

His shrug was a beat too late. 'The team can manage without me.'

'But you're the manager. Are you supposed to be supervising?'

His back was to her now and he spoke as he reached for milk and sugar. 'I have a satellite phone. I can stay in touch.' He turned, and his green eyes regarded her steadily. 'You should know that, Senator. After all, you'll be running the whole country from here.'

It was a not-so-subtle dig—and she realised that Jack probably resented her sudden arrival.

She said, 'I suppose you're wondering how a federal

senator can retreat into the outback without reneging on her responsibilities.'

'Not at all. I leave politicking to politicians.' Jack's face was as unreadable as a poker player's as he poured tea into a mug. 'Do you take milk? Sugar?'

'Thank you.' She helped herself to a dash of milk and half a spoon of sugar. 'I hope I haven't spoiled too many of your plans.'

'Most plans are easy enough to change.' Jack sat and, now that he was level with Lizzie, she was reacquainted with the superior breadth of his shoulders.

He looked across the table at her, trapping her in his steady gaze. 'That goes for you, too, Senator. No one's holding you here if you find that this place doesn't suit you.'

Something in his gaze set fine tuning-fork vibrations inside her. Quickly, she looked down at her mug. 'Please, you mustn't keep calling me Senator.'

'What should I call you? Elizabeth?'

'My family and friends call me Lizzie.'

'Lizzie?' Jack repeated her name without shifting his gaze from her face. 'Now that's a surprise.'

'Why?'

His mouth twitched as he stirred sugar into black tea. 'Seems to me, a woman called Lizzie is a very different kettle of fish from an Elizabeth.'

'Really? How?' As soon as the question was out Lizzie regretted it. It wasn't appropriate for her to show so much interest in this young man's theories about women and their names. And yet, she was desperately curious to hear his answer.

'When I think of Elizabeth, I think of the Queen,' Jack said.

'My mother would be pleased to hear that. It's why she chose Elizabeth as my name.'

'She named you after the Queen?'

'Yes. She named all her daughters after strong women. I have a younger sister Jackie, named after Jackie Onassis, and then there's Scarlett, named after Scarlet O'Hara.'

'Yeah?' Jack chuckled. 'No maternal pressure or anything.' He lolled back in his chair, legs stretched under the table. The man sure had a talent for looking relaxed. 'Your mother must be proud of you. A federal senator. That's a pretty big deal.'

'Yes, I'm sure she is proud.'

'But she still calls you Lizzie.'

Lizzie… *Cara*…

With a wistful pang Lizzie remembered her mother's tearful reaction to the news she'd shared just last week, when she'd flown back to Italy, to her hometown of Monta Correnti. Her mother's tears had been happy, of course, and accompanied by fierce and wonderful hugs.

Lisa Firenzi was thrilled that her eldest daughter was about to become a mother at last, and she'd been surprisingly OK with the unexpected news that her grandchild's father was an unknown donor. But then, Lisa Firenzi had never bowed to convention.

Like mother, like daughter…

Lizzie took a sip of her tea, which was hot and strong, just as she liked it, and she pushed aside memories of the end of her visit home, and the unhappy family row that had erupted.

Instead, she asked Jack, 'Why do you think Lizzie is so different from Elizabeth? What kind of woman is a Lizzie?'

Jack laughed out loud and the flash in his eyes was most definitely wicked. 'I'm afraid I don't know you well enough to answer that.'

For heaven's sake, he was flirting with her. She had to stop this now. She was most definitely not looking for any kind of relationship. Apart from the fact that she'd given up on men, she was pregnant, for heaven's sake. Besides, Jack was probably the kind of man who flirted with any available female.

Lizzie froze him with her most cutting glare. It was time to get serious. Really serious. She hadn't come to the outback for a holiday, and she certainly hadn't come here for romance. She had a stack of paperwork to get through and she should set Jack Lewis straight. Now.

And yet…she couldn't help wondering…who was she really? An Elizabeth? Or a Lizzie?

A small frown settled between Jack's brows and he stood abruptly. 'We should talk about meals,' he said. 'The pantry's well stocked and so is the cold room, but we're the only ones here to do the cooking, so—'

'We?' Lizzie interrupted, somewhat startled. 'You're not expecting me to cook, are you?'

He slid a sideways glance to the big country stove, then back to Lizzie. 'Excuse me, Senator. Perhaps you weren't aware that lesser mortals actually prepare their own meals?'

'Of course I know that,' she snapped, aware that he probably planned to call her Senator whenever he wanted to put her down.

Jack narrowed his eyes at her. 'Can you recognise one end of a saucepan from another?'

She rolled her eyes to the ceiling to show her exasperation, but, truth was, in recent years she'd been far too busy to dally with anything remotely domesticated. Admittedly, since she'd become pregnant, she'd been conscientious about breakfast—making a smoothie from yoghurt and fruit—but her PA brought her a salad from the deli for lunch, and her diary was filled with evening engagements—charity functions, political dinners, business meetings—so she often ate out.

On the few occasions she ate at home, the meals had mostly been takeaway, eaten at her desk with little attention to taste or texture. She couldn't remember the last time she'd eaten alone with a man in a private home.

'I don't have time for cooking.' Lizzie added a dash of ice to her tone.

Not in the least intimidated, Jack leaned his hips against a cupboard and eyed her steadily. 'Then you'll have to risk your digestion with my cooking.'

'Is that a threat?'

His eyes held the glimmer of menace. 'I guess you'll soon find out, won't you? Otherwise, you could go solo and make your own meals. No skin off my nose. Or we could take turns at the stove and share what we cook.'

'Share?' Lizzie set her mug down before she spilled its contents. She hadn't shared a house, taking turns in the kitchen, since her carefree university days.

Back then, when she'd shared a house and a kitchen, she'd also fallen in love. With Mitch.

Her mind flashed an unbidden memory of her younger, laughing self, teaching Mitch to test spaghetti by throwing it against the kitchen wall to see if it stuck. As always, he'd had a better idea, and they'd shared a spaghetti strand between their linked mouths, eating until their lips met. And then, of course, they'd kissed…and, quite probably, they'd gone to bed. She'd been so madly in love back then.

But it was such a long time ago.

'No worries.' Jack gave her a crooked grin. 'I'm no chef, but I guess I can look after the cooking. I hope you like steak.'

'Steak's fine,' Lizzie said, and then, to her astonishment, she found herself adding, 'but I'm sure I could brush up on a few old recipes.'

When Jack looked uncertain, she supplied her credentials. 'After all, my mother owns a restaurant.'

'A restaurant?' His eyes widened, suitably impressed. 'Where?'

'In Monta Correnti. In Italy.'

'An Italian restaurant!' Jack sent her an eye-rolling grin and rubbed his stomach. 'I love Italian tucker. I bet the talent for cooking runs in your family.' His grin deepened. 'And here I was thinking you were just a pretty face.'

As Lizzie unpacked her suitcases she refused to think about Jack Lewis. She especially refused to think about his throwaway line about her pretty face.

For heaven's sake, he was a young man, barely thirty, and she was pregnant and practically middle-aged, and she'd long ago learned to ignore comments about her looks.

Female politicians were fair game for the media, and from the moment she'd hit parliament journalists had paid far too much attention to her appearance, her dress sense, and her hairstyles. It had been beyond infuriating.

Since Lizzie's university days, she'd had her heart set on working hard to better the lives of ordinary, everyday Australians, but the reporters only seemed to notice what she was wearing, or which man she was dating.

There'd been one infamous photo, early in her career, of her coming out of a restaurant, arm in arm with a male colleague. Her hair was loose, blowing in the wind, and she was wearing a shortish skirt with knee-high Italian leather boots. The boots were dark red, and the photo had found its way onto the front page of every metropolitan daily in the nation.

"Boots and all" the headlines had announced. It was as if she'd dropped IQ points simply because she'd worn something sexy.

After that, Lizzie had chosen to keep her hair in a tidy bun and to dress sedately and she'd schooled herself to ignore the unwanted attention of the press gallery.

Jack's comment was no different. It was water off a duck's back.

Of course it was.

She concentrated on colour-coding her clothing as she hung it in the old-fashioned wardrobe with an oval mirror on the door. Her undergarments and nightwear went into the Baltic pine chest of drawers.

She arranged the ten good books she'd brought on her desk, and set up her laptop, checked that the Internet connection worked—yes, thank heavens—and downloaded a raft of emails from her office.

Out of habit, she answered them promptly, although she would have loved to ignore them today and to wander down the hall to the old-fashioned bathroom, to take a long soak in the deep, claw-foot tub she'd spied there. Just as she would have loved to take a little nap on the big white bed, with the French doors open to catch the breeze blowing in from the paddocks.

She couldn't slacken off on her very first day. It was important to prove to herself and to her colleagues that this month-long retreat would not stop her from working.

With business emails completed, Lizzie sent a quick message of thanks to Kate Burton, telling her that she'd arrived safely. She considered gently chiding Kate for not warning her about Jack's youth, but she decided that even a gentle protest might give Kate the wrong idea.

She also sent a quick note to her mother and another,

warmer message to her cousin Isabella in Monta Correnti, telling her about the move to Savannah.

During Lizzie's latest trip to Italy, Isabella had surprised everyone by announcing her engagement to Maximilliano Di Rossi. But to Lizzie's dismay, the exciting news had been rather overshadowed by the terrible animosity that flared up, worse than ever, between her mother and Isabella's father, Luca.

There'd been ongoing tensions between the two families for decades now, fuelled by the fierce rivalry between their restaurants, "Sorella" and "Rosa", which stood next door to each other in Monta Correnti.

Lizzie, however, had always been close friends with Isabella, and she was determined to keep in touch with her now as an important step in her plan to build bridges across the family divide.

In her private life and her public life Lizzie Green planned to become a stress-free zone…

And with her duties accomplished, the big white bed still beckoned.

Really, she found herself asking, what was the harm? She'd been fighting tiredness ever since she'd first become pregnant—and there'd been an embarrassing occasion when she'd nodded off during a senate enquiry into the cost of roadworks in new mining areas.

Now, she was here in one of the remotest corners of the big empty outback, amazingly free to adjust her schedule in any way she liked, and next to no one would be any the wiser.

After years of relentless hard work and a punishing schedule, the sudden freedom was scary.

But it was real.

Wow.

Yes, she really was free. Out here, no one would know

or care if Senator Elizabeth Green took a long, relaxing bath in the middle of the afternoon. There were no journalists lurking outside the homestead, and Lizzie was free to contemplate the miracle happening inside her.

As always, her spirits lifted the instant she thought about the tiny little baby growing in her womb.

She was so, so glad she'd gone along with her plan, in spite of all the worry, and the doubts voiced by her friends.

'A sperm donor, Lizzie? You've got to be joking.'

Her girlfriends hadn't understood at first, and Lizzie couldn't really blame them. For years it hadn't bothered her that she was the only woman in her circle of friends who was still single and babyless. She'd been almost smug, proud that she was an independent thinker, a New Age woman who didn't bow down to the pressure to follow the crowd. She was focused on a higher calling.

Unfortunately, the smugness hadn't lasted.

At thirty-eight pushing thirty-nine, almost overnight, something had clicked inside her. She'd been gripped by a sudden, deep and painful yearning for the precious, warm weight of a baby in her arms. Not a friend's baby. Not a niece or a nephew.

Her baby.

The longing had become so powerful it had pressed against Lizzie's heart, becoming a constant ache, impossible to ignore and she'd faced the alarming truth that her body was a ticking time bomb…counting down, down, down…to a lonely and childless future…

Of course, the lack of a potential father for her baby had posed a hiccup. The scars left first by Mitch, and several years later by Toby, were deep and painful. Still.

Even so, Lizzie had tried dating. Truly, she had tried. But all the decent guys were already married, and she wasn't prepared to settle for Mr Good Enough, and there was no way she would leap into a convenient marriage just to have a baby. Where was the morality in that?

Besides, Lizzie had learned at her mother's knee that a woman could embrace independence and single motherhood with dignity and flair.

So she'd settled on a sperm bank, but it had taken twelve nail-biting months before a viable pregnancy was confirmed. By that time, Lizzie had been so fraught and nervous that Kate Burton had kindly insisted that she spend some time at her outback cattle station, where she could enjoy being pregnant out of the spotlight.

Lizzie had accepted with gratitude.

She knew only too well that eventually there would be questions, and all kinds of fuss about the sperm-bank decision. People would say that she'd kissed her political career goodbye, but for now she wanted to give her baby its best chance to be born healthy. Already, she loved it fiercely.

After the birth, she'd find a way to continue her career and raise her child.

Lizzie Green always found a way.

But right now, on this sunny autumn afternoon, she was a forty year old woman, pregnant for the first time, and feeling just a little lonely. And more than anything she was tired.

So why shouldn't she take that bath? If for no other reason than because she needed to get rid of the gritty red dust between her toes. Already she could picture the soothing ritual of running water, adding a swoosh of the scented salts that Kate had left. A glug of luxurious oil, then sliding down for a long soak.

And then afterwards, why not a nap?

* * *

At six o'clock, Jack tapped his knuckles on the door to Lizzie's room to tell her that dinner was ready.

When there was no answer he cleared his throat and called, 'Senator Green?' And then, another knock. 'Lizzie?'

Still there was no answer, and he wondered if she'd gone for a walk.

He'd come to her room via the veranda, so it was a simple matter to lean over the railing to scan the yard and the home paddock, but he saw no sign of her.

Surely she hadn't wandered off? Damn it. Was she going to be a nuisance on her very first day here?

He supposed there was no point in searching elsewhere without checking her room first, so he stepped through the open French doors, and his heart almost stopped beating when he saw her.

Asleep. Like a modern-day Sleeping Beauty.

Jack knew exactly what he should do—turn smartly on his heel, march straight back out of the room and knock again loudly, and he should keep on knocking or calling until the senator heard him and woke up.

Pigs might fly.

No way on this earth could he move. His feet were bolted to the floor, and his eyes were glued to Lizzie as she lay there.

She'd changed into soft and faded low-rise jeans and a pale green, sleeveless top with a low neck and little ruffles down the front. The way she was lying, curled on her side, exposed a good six inches of bare midriff.

Hey, senator, you're not so bad when you're asleep.

Not so bad? Who was he kidding?

Sleep hadn't only stolen Lizzie's haughtiness; it had left her defenceless and vulnerable. Out-of-this-world sexy.

With the attention of an artist commissioned to paint her portrait, Jack took careful note of details.

The soft light filtering through the curtains washed her with warm shadows, highlighting the intricate pattern of fine veins on her eyelids, the dusky curve of her lashes, and her dark hair rippling like water over her pillow.

Her mouth was a lush, full-blown rose, and the scooped neckline of her blouse revealed a little gold cross winking between the voluptuous swell of her breasts. His hands ached to touch her, to trace the cello-like dip and curve of her waist and hip.

Even her bare feet resting with one pressed against the other were neatly arched and sexy.

Far out. He had to get out of here fast. This sleeping beauty might look like every temptation known to man, but he knew damn well that the minute she woke she would morph straight back into the officious and cold city senator. So not the kind of woman he'd ever get involved with.

Jack forced himself to take a step back. And another. Problem was, he was still watching Lizzie instead of where he was going, and he backed into a chest of drawers, sending a hairbrush clattering to the floor.

She was instantly awake, sitting up quickly, dark hair flying about her shoulders, eyes and mouth wide with shock.

'I'm sorry.' Jack threw up his hands, protesting his innocence. 'Don't scream. It's OK.'

She was breathing rapidly, clearly frightened and disoriented, but even so she clung to her dignity.

'I'm not in the habit of screaming,' she said haughtily, while she tugged at the bottom of her blouse with both hands in a bid to close the gap of bare midriff.

No, Jack thought wryly as he bent to retrieve her silver-backed hairbrush and set it on the chest. Of course she wasn't a screamer. She was too cool. Too tough.

'I was trying to call you from the veranda, but you were

out like a light,' he said, forcing himself backwards towards the door. 'I just wanted to let you know that dinner's ready when you are.'

'Dinner? Already?' She sent a hasty glance to the fading light outside, then frowned as she reached for the wristwatch on the bedside table. When she saw the time, she let out a huff of annoyance. 'I've been asleep for hours.'

'Half your luck.'

Clearly Lizzie didn't agree. Already she was off the bed, shuffling her feet into shoes while tying her hair into a tight, neat knot. 'Your steaks will be overcooked,' she said.

'At ease, Lizzie.'

She went still and frowned at him and Jack wondered what she would do if she knew how amazing she looked at that moment. In the shadowy twilight, with her arms raised to fix her hair, her breasts were wonderfully rounded and lifted, and the luscious gap of creamy skin at her waist was on show once more.

Jack forced his gaze to the floor. It was clearly too long since he'd had a girlfriend.

'We're not having steaks tonight,' he said. 'There's a stroganoff and it's simmering away nicely, so you've no need to rush.'

'Stroganoff?' Lizzie's eyes widened. 'You're serving stroganoff?'

'It's no big deal.' Jack shrugged, and began to head back along the veranda, calling over his shoulder, 'I'll see you in the kitchen. No hurry. Whenever you're ready.'

In the meantime he would go chop firewood, although it wasn't yet winter. Or he'd make a phone call to his dentist and volunteer to have all his teeth drilled, even though they were cavity-free. Anything to take his mind off his sexy, out-of-bounds houseguest.

* * *

To Lizzie's surprise, the stroganoff was really good. The beef was tender, the mushrooms plump and sweet, and the sauce super-smooth and tasty. She found that she was hungry—ravenous, in fact, with a new interest in food that had begun when she'd reached the end of her first trimester. As soon as her morning sickness had stopped, her appetite had blossomed.

Along with her libido. Which no doubt explained the difficulty she was having keeping her eyes off Jack. She didn't understand how she could find a man who'd slaved over a kitchen stove so incredibly attractive.

Lizzie respected successful, career-driven men, powerful politicians, or business magnates at the top of the corporate ladder. An unambitious cowboy, who managed a remote cattle property for an imperious old lady, held no appeal whatsoever.

And yet…she'd never seen blue jeans sit so attractively on a man, and Jack's shoulders were truly sensational. As for the easy way he moved and the lively sparkle in his eyes…and his smile…

He made her feel girly and soft.

Clearly, pregnancy hormones had depleted her common sense and awakened her earthier instincts.

It was an unsettling problem, and it wasn't going away.

'This is an excellent meal,' she admitted, in a bid to keep her mind on the food. 'I'm impressed.'

From across the table, Jack accepted her praise with a nonchalant smile. 'Glad you like it.' He drank deeply from a glass of beer.

'I suppose it was just a little something you threw together?'

'More or less.'

Lizzie didn't return Jack's smile. Her enjoyment of the

meal was somewhat spoiled by her competitive instincts. Already, she was wondering how she could match Jack's culinary efforts when it was her turn to cook, and she wished she could remember the finer points of her mother's favourite recipes.

'I've heard that country folk are exceptionally resourceful,' she said. 'I imagine you're probably a mechanic, a cook, a cattleman and a businessman all rolled into one.'

'Something like that.' Jack's green eyes narrowed. 'That's how most city people see us, at any rate. Jack of all trades and master of none.'

Lizzie was surprised that easy-going Jack was suddenly touchy. Clearly she'd hit a raw nerve.

Practised at calming touchy politicians, she said, 'A senator has to be a bit like that, too. Economist one day, social worker the next. You get to be a minor expert in one hundred and one areas of policy.' A moment later, she asked, 'Have you always lived in the outback?'

Jack took his time answering her. 'Pretty much. Except for the years I spent at boarding school.'

'And did you grow up always wanting to work on the land?'

This question should have been perfectly harmless, but again it seemed to annoy Jack. Leaning forward, elbows on the table, he twisted his glass between his hands. 'Did you grow up always wanting to be a politician?'

'Oh—' Lizzie wasn't normally thrown by sudden about-turns, but tonight she was off her game. She responded too quickly, 'Not really. Politics was something I sort of fell into.'

Jack's eyes widened with understandable surprise.

Unhappily, Lizzie set her knife and fork neatly together on her empty plate, sank back in her chair and let out an involuntary sigh. Why on earth had she made such a revealing confession to this man? She gave a dismissive wave of her hand. 'Everything changed when I went to university.'

He sent her a teasing grin. 'Don't tell me that you fell in with the wrong crowd?'

'I suppose you could say that,' she replied icily. 'I met a group of hardworking, committed idealists.'

Jack pulled a face as if to show that he wasn't impressed. Then he rose, and took their plates to the sink.

'Well…thanks for dinner.' Lizzie stood, too. It was time to get back to the work she'd missed while she'd napped. 'The stroganoff was delicious.'

'Hey,' he called as she headed for the door, 'Don't hard-working, committed idealists help with the dishes?'

Lizzie's cheeks grew hot. She hadn't given dishwashing a thought. Now she imagined standing with Jack at the sink, side by side, chatting cosily, possibly brushing against each other while they washed and dried their dishes.

'I'll wash up when I cook tomorrow night,' she said, and, without another word, she made a dignified, if hasty, exit.

Instead of watching TV as he did most nights, Jack spent the evening in the machinery shed, tinkering with the old station truck. The brakes were dodgy and needed fixing, and he seized the excuse to stay well clear of the home-stead, well clear of Lizzie.

Unfortunately, staying clear of the senator didn't stop him from thinking about her. He kept remembering the way she'd looked when she was sleeping, kept thinking about her mouth, and how it would taste if he kissed her.

When he kissed her.

He was an A-grade fool.

He should be remembering how the senator turned starchy as soon as she woke, and the snooty way her lush mouth tightened when he asked her to do a simple thing like help with the dishes. Elizabeth Green was light years away from the kind of girl he was used to. She didn't even belong on a cattle property.

He couldn't imagine why Kate Burton had sent her here. Surely she must have known that Lizzie wouldn't fit in?

Jack had lived in the outback all his life and everyone he knew, even the hoity-toity grazier's wives, pitched in to lend a hand. On a working cattle property, people pulled their weight with everything from opening gates and helping with the dishes, to cooking, gardening, caring for children, mending a fence, or joining the cattle muster. Jack could remember one occasion when his mother had even helped to fight bushfires.

If the senator thought he was going to run around waiting on her, she had another think coming. She'd waltzed onto Savannah at an extremely inconvenient time, and she certainly couldn't expect kid-glove treatment.

If he had his way, he'd bring her down a peg or two.

Problem was, even though Lizzie was out of place here, and even though she was bossy and citified and bloody annoying, she *was* incredibly sexy. Maddeningly so. Those lips of hers and those alluring curves were driving Jack crazy. Already, after half a day.

An entire month of her presence on Savannah was going to be torture.

If Jack thought it would work, he'd ignore Kate's request to play host to Lizzie, and he'd ring the contract mustering plant on his satellite phone and offer to trade places with Bill Jervis, his cook.

Bill was sixty, and a grandfather, and he could keep an eye on Lizzie Green as easily as Jack could, and he could prepare top-class meals for her every night. Jack, on the other hand, could be out on the muster with the stockmen. They had a difficult task, clearing three thousand head of cattle out of some very rough country, and his intimate knowledge of the Savannah terrain would be a definite asset.

The swapping scheme was beautiful in its simplicity. There was only one problem with it. Jack might be a good stockman, but he'd have a mutiny on his hands if he tried to deprive the ringers of Bill's cooking.

Which brought him back to square one—he had no choice but to stay put and to grin and bear Lizzie Green's presence here.

It was ten o'clock when he left the truck's innards lying in pieces on the machinery shed floor and went to the laundry to scrub off the worst of his grime. The laundry was a simple wooden lean-to attached to the back of the house—a very basic and functional bachelor affair. Tonight, however, it was filled with white linen clothes soaking in sparkling suds, and wispy bits of lingerie dangled from a tiny line suspended above it.

Jack groaned as the fantasies fuelled by those scant scraps of fabric caused a whole new set of problems.

CHAPTER THREE

THE strident laughter of kookaburras woke Lizzie. Disoriented, she lay still, staring about her, taking in the soft grey morning light that crept through an unfamiliar window. Slowly, she remembered her arrival at Savannah yesterday, and why she'd come here.

She smelled bacon frying, which meant Jack was up.

Dismayed, she washed and dressed and hurried to the kitchen. It would be her turn to cook dinner this evening and already the task was looming in her mind as The Great Kitchen Challenge. She wanted to catch Jack before he took off for some far-flung corner of the property, to ask him about the contents of Savannah's pantry.

He was still at the stove, fortunately, tending to a frying pan, and looking far more appealing than any man had a right to look at such an early hour.

He was wearing a blue cotton shirt, faded from much washing, and old jeans torn at the knee. His fair hair was backlit by the morning sun and his skin was brown and weather-beaten, and he looked astonishingly real, and vitally alive. Impossibly attractive.

But I don't want to be attracted. I can't believe I'm reacting this way. It's bizarre.

He turned and smiled, and Lizzie's insides folded.

'Morning, Senator.'

'Good morning, Jack.' Good heavens. She sounded ridiculously breathless.

'Hope you slept well?'

'Quite well, thank you.'

She cast a deliberately cool glance at the contents of the frying pan and suppressed an urge to enquire about Jack's cholesterol levels.

'You're welcome to share this,' he said.

'No, thanks.' She gave a theatrical shudder. 'I usually have yoghurt and fruit.'

'Suit yourself,' he said smoothly. 'The fruit bowl's on the table. Feel free to take whatever you like. I'm pretty sure Bill keeps yoghurt in the cold room.'

'The cold room?'

With a lazy thumbing gesture, Jack pointed to a door in the opposite wall. 'Through there.'

Good heavens. What kind of host expected his guests to hunt for their own meals? Lizzie was distinctly put out as he turned off the heat and loaded up his plate, leaving her to march into the huge cold room in search of yoghurt.

Admittedly, the cold room was very well organised, and she found, not only a small tub of biodynamic berry yoghurt, but the cuts of meat she needed for the evening's meal.

'I've made coffee,' Jack said, sending her a smile when she returned. 'And there's still plenty in the pot.'

'I'm afraid I can't drink coffee.'

His eyebrows rose high. 'You don't like it?'

'Not—at the moment.' The doctors had warned Lizzie to avoid coffee while she was pregnant. 'I'll make tea,' she said, guessing he was unlikely to offer. Then, 'So what are your plans for the day?'

'I'll be bleeding the brakes on the old truck we use to cart feed around the property.'

'Bleeding brakes? That sounds tricky.'

'It is, actually. I decided to give the truck an overhaul while the men are away, and I started last night, but the brakes are even worse than I thought.' His green gaze held hers. 'I'm afraid I'm going to need a hand.'

Lizzie frowned. 'But there's no one left here to help you, is there?'

Across the table, he flashed a grin. 'That's why I was hoping you'd offer to help.'

'Me?' Lizzie's jaw dropped so quickly she was surprised it didn't crack.

'I'd really appreciate it.'

Stunned, she shook her head. '*I* can't help you. I'm far too busy, and I don't know the first thing about trucks. I've never even changed a tyre.'

'You don't need to *know* anything. You just have to press the brake pedal a few times.'

Clearly, Jack was one of those people who thought politicians only worked when parliament was in session. Lizzie was used to colleagues who treated her heavy workload with due reverence, but Jack didn't give a hoot about her investigations into fairer private health incentives.

'I have a mountain of important documents to read through this morning.' *And I have to spend this afternoon cooking*.

'You could spare a few minutes.'

Shocked, Lizzie stared at him, angry at his lack of respect. That is, she wanted to be angry. She intended to be angry, but his naughty-boy smile was like sun thawing frost.

She heard herself saying, feebly, 'I—I suppose I might be able to spare ten minutes. No more.'

Which was how she found herself in the machinery

shed a quarter of an hour later, balanced on the front bumper of a rusty old truck, breathing in diesel, while she stared helplessly at a bewildering tangle of metal cylinders, knobs, pipes and rubber hoses.

'I have to get fluid through the system and air out of the lines,' Jack said.

'So what do I have to do?'

'I'll need your help just as soon as I've poured this fluid down the brake line.'

'Where's the brake line?'

'Over there to the right, next to the carburettor.'

Lizzie hadn't a clue where the carburettor was, but she couldn't help admiring the concentration on Jack's face as he poured the fluid, very carefully, not spilling a drop.

That done, he told her to hop behind the wheel, ready to work the brakes, and then he promptly disappeared beneath the truck.

Fine prickles darted over Lizzie's skin as she watched him. There was something so very earthy and unsettling about seeing a grown man—a gorgeous, broad-shouldered, lean-hipped grown man, no less—on his back, on the ground, easing himself under a mass of machinery.

Jack's head and shoulders disappeared first, and she found herself staring at his torso and legs...at the bare tanned skin showing through the tear in his jeans—not a designer tear, but a proper work-worn rip—at the battered leather plait threaded through his belt loops...and the very masculine bulge beneath the zip in the centre seam.

Her mouth went dry as she actually imagined lying there beside him, on top of him, under him, their bodies intimately entwined.

'Right,' Jack called. 'Press the brake down steadily with an even force.'

'Oh.'

Caught out, she had to scramble to get into the truck's cabin.

'OK,' she called, a flustered minute later. 'I'm pressing the brake now.'

'Sing out "down", when you've pressed it as far as it will go. And then take it off when I call "up".'

It wasn't easy to depress the brake fully. Lizzie had to sit on the very edge of the seat, but at last she called, 'Down!'

It was ages before Jack called, 'OK. Up!'

Relieved, she let the brake off, but then Jack called, 'Can you do that again?' And the process was repeated over and over, while he patiently tested and retested the first brake, and then the brakes connected to each of the truck's wheels.

She couldn't believe he'd dragged her all the way down here just to call out 'down'. The process took much longer than ten minutes, and she was angry about the precious time she was wasting...

And yet, to her immense surprise, she actually enjoyed the strange back-and-forth communication with his disembodied voice. She liked the sense of teamwork...and she had to admit that brakes *were* vitally important... Men's lives relied on them.

Besides...she kept picturing Jack on his back beneath the massive vehicle...kept remembering how breathtaking he'd looked down there.

Oh, no. Not again.

How could she be obsessing about a man who was at least ten years younger than her? A man who had no idea that she was pregnant?

It was all very disturbing. And surprising. This time yesterday she'd been chairing a last-minute face-to-face meeting to discuss the Renewal Energy Amendment Bill.

Today she was perched behind the wheel of a truck in an outback machinery shed, breathing in diesel fumes, and having a disjointed conversation with a man lying beneath the vehicle.

It was almost as if she'd been teleported to another planet.

Finally, Jack shouted, 'OK, that's it. All good.'

Relieved, Lizzie scrambled down from the truck, and Jack slid out from beneath it, wiping blackened hands on an old rag. He jumped to his feet with easy grace.

'Thanks,' he said. 'I couldn't have done that without your help. You were brilliant.'

He was looking into her eyes and his smile was so genuine, Lizzie became flustered and dismissive. 'Don't be silly. It was nothing.'

Jack laughed. 'I suppose you're used to putting your foot down.'

Her smile stiffened. 'It's a very necessary part of my job. Now, if you'll excuse me, I must get straight back to that job.'

'By all means, Senator. I'll walk with you to the house. I need to make a phone call to Kate Burton.'

Walking with Jack hadn't been part of her plan. She'd been hoping to escape his knowing smile, and those ripped jeans, the rumpled shirt, and the smear of grease on his jaw.

As they left the shed and emerged into dazzling sunlight Jack asked in a conversational tone, 'So how long have you known Kate?'

'Oh, for quite a few years.' Lizzie couldn't help smiling. 'Kate's hard to miss. She's involved in so many organisations. Quite a mover and shaker. On the national board of several charities. She got me onside to help with funding for additional places in aged care.'

Jack grinned. 'That sounds like her cup of tea.'

'Actually, it was a tall order. We needed to increase the

budget for the aging by a third, but Treasury was blocking it. In the end I had to get support from both houses to allow the passage of a new bill. Kate was very grateful.'

'No doubt.' Jack's voice was strangely rough, and his mouth had twisted into a complicated smile.

'What about you, Jack? How long have you known her?'

He shrugged. 'Since I was a kid. She and my mother have always been friends.'

Lizzie expected further explanation, but they'd reached the homestead steps.

'I'd better let you get to work,' he said, moving ahead of her, taking the steps two at a time, then swiftly disappearing inside, and leaving Lizzie to wonder if she'd said something wrong.

In his study, Jack raked a shaky hand through his hair.

He picked up the phone, dropped it down again, paced to the window and looked out, shocked by the confusion churning inside him. He fancied Lizzie like crazy, but she was the last woman on the planet he should chase.

Why would he want to? It didn't make sense. Why would an outback cowboy even dream of getting together with a high-profile federal senator, who had the power to affect the course of their nation?

She wasn't remotely his type. She was ambitious, and driven. The kind of person he'd always steered clear of. Too much like his father.

Jack's stomach clenched tighter as he thought about his old man.

Ambition, boy. That's what you need. A man's nothing without ambition.

Sure, Dad.

To please his old man, Jack had chosen his life's goal

at the age of six. Together they'd watched Air Force
training exercises—sleek, super-sophisticated monsters
ripping across the outback skies—and Jack had decided
that as soon as he finished school, he would be in the
cockpit of a fighter jet.

To impress his dad, he'd spent his boyhood trying to
excel in the usual outback activities, but no matter how
many pony races or calf-roping events he'd won, his father
had always found something to criticise.

Just remembering the boxing lessons he'd taken sent a
wave of resentment through Jack. He'd never satisfied his
old man. He was constantly criticised for not having the
killer instinct, for standing back if an opponent slipped, or
for holding back on a knockout.

He'd put up with it all, however, because he knew that
one day he'd finally make his father proud.

Then he'd sat the recruitment exams. Jack had known
he had the necessary co-ordination and fitness, and he'd
scored good grades in the required subjects, so he'd gone
into the final tests brimming with confidence.

He'd come out devastated.

He'd passed every section with ease, except the most
important of all—the psych test.

The recruiting officers had been diplomatic, but Jack
got the message. He wasn't cut out to fly their devastat-
ing weapons into battle. They wanted someone with a
ruthless streak, with hard arrogance and a get-out-of-my-
way attitude…

The kind of man his father had pushed him to be… The
kind of man he could never be…

It had taken Jack years to accept this, and to finally be
comfortable in his own skin. Now, his awareness of his
strengths and weaknesses only made it plain as day that he

and Lizzie were polar opposites. He had no doubt that she'd trampled on people as she scaled the heights of parliament.

She was pushy and powerful. She had to be. OK, maybe she was driven by an urge to help people, but maybe she was also just hungry for success.

Bottom line—they had nothing in common. He was a strumming guitar. Lizzie was the whole brass band. Why was he lusting after a woman like that? And why the hell couldn't he simply talk himself out of it?

By six o'clock, Lizzie was ready to crawl into bed. Instead she had to face a mountain of washing-up.

She was out of practice at this cooking caper, and she'd gone overboard, of course.

Inspired by fond memories of her Grandmother Rosa's ossobucco in a heavenly vegetable sauce, she'd thrown herself into the task. She'd been so sure it would be the perfect meal to impress Jack, so she'd hunted on the Internet for a recipe that closely matched her memories of Rosa's dish, and she'd followed it to the letter.

The first part hadn't been too bad. She'd already found the meat she needed in the homestead's cold room and she'd tied string around each ossobucco, then lightly floured them on both sides, but not around the edges.

While they were browning, she'd cut zucchinis, carrots, onion and celery—all of which she'd found in a surprisingly well-maintained kitchen garden at the back of the house.

With the casserole in the oven, however, Lizzie had begun on the special vegetable sauce that had made her grandmother's dish out of the ordinary. Four different vegetables—peas, beans, carrots and celery—all had to go into separate bowls of cold water and soak for half an hour. Each vegetable then had to be boiled in its own pot, then they were blended together before being added as a smooth sauce to the casserole.

Honestly, Lizzie knew it was ridiculous to go to such lengths for a simple evening meal with Jack Lewis. He'd managed to throw together last night's meal with a minimum of fuss, and he'd only used one pot, for heaven's sake. She, on the other hand, had used practically every saucepan and dish in the kitchen.

With too much to fit in the dishwasher she was still up to her elbows in detergent suds when she heard Jack's footsteps approaching.

'Honey, I'm home!' he called in a pseudo-American accent, rippling with humour.

She spun around, outrageously pleased to see him fresh from the shower, damp strands of dark blond hair flopping onto his forehead, and smelling of sexy aftershave.

He was smiling and he looked so genuinely pleased to see her that her heart seemed to tilt in her chest.

'How's the truck?'

Jack smiled. 'I took it for a test-drive this afternoon and it runs as smoothly as a sewing machine. The brakes are perfect.' He sent a curious glance to the stove. 'I'm faint with hunger, and that smells amazing. Is it Italian?'

'Yes.' Lizzie took a breath to calm down. 'It's ossobucco.' *Oh, dear.* She sounded far too proud of herself, didn't she?

'Ossobucco?' Jack's eyebrows lifted. 'That's authentic. Did you have any trouble finding everything you needed?'

'Not at all.' She wondered how he could look at her with such thrilling intensity and discuss food at the same time. 'There are so many different cuts of meat in the cold room, and all sorts of vegetables in the garden.'

'All thanks to Bill,' Jack admitted.

'Is he the cook who's out with the mustering team?'

'The one and only.' Jack saw the huge pile of dishes in front of her. 'Hey, you knew you only had to cook one meal tonight, didn't you?'

Lizzie bit her lip. 'You weren't supposed to see this mess. I wanted it all cleared up before we ate.'

'But what have you been up to? Cooking for a whole week?'

'No,' she said tightly, turning back to the sink, highly embarrassed by the amount of mess she'd made.

Jack snagged a tea towel. 'I'll give you a hand.'

'No!' This time she almost snapped at him. 'Please, don't bother. I—I'll have these dishes done in no time. Dinner won't be ready for another ten minutes, or so. Why don't you go and—and—'

'Count kookaburras?' he suggested with a knowing smile.

'Watch a bit of television,' she supplied lamely.

Shrugging, he crossed the kitchen, opened the refrigerator and selected a beer. 'I'll feed the dog,' he said as he snapped the top off the beer.

Lizzie felt strangely deflated when he left the room. Lips compressed, she finished the dishes and set the cleared end of the table, took the casserole from the oven, and cut the strings from around the meat before setting it aside to rest.

When Jack wandered back, he was carrying a dusty bottle of red wine. 'I found this in the cellar. I thought your meal deserved something better than beer.'

Lizzie forced a smile.

'You'll join me, won't you?' he said, reaching into an overhead cupboard for wine glasses.

'Um…I'm not drinking alcohol at the moment.'

Jack's green eyes widened. 'This retreat of yours requires abstinence?'

'Yes.'

With a puzzled grin, he held out the bottle. 'But this is a great vintage, and it's Italian vino.'

'I'm sure it's lovely, Jack.' She forced lightness into her voice. 'But you can't tempt me to the dark side. I won't have wine tonight, thanks.'

He turned the bottle in his hands, frowning at the label. 'I don't want to drink it alone. Guess I'll stick with beer.'

'I'm sorry. Normally, I'd love a glass of wine, but I'm—'

The word *pregnant* died on Lizzie's lips.

Annoyed with the situation, she picked up a fork from the table and rubbed at it against a tea towel as if she were removing a spot.

'No worries.' Jack was as easy-going as ever.

But Lizzie *was* worried. She shouldn't feel bad simply because she hadn't told Jack about her pregnancy. He didn't need to know. It wasn't any of his business. Except…unfortunately, she knew there was another reason she was clinging to her secret.

Her news would kill the playful warmth in his eyes, and, for reasons that made no sense at all, she didn't want to break the bewildering thread of attraction that thrummed between them. She hadn't felt anything like it for ages. She didn't want to feel anything like it. She'd deliberately distanced herself from such feelings.

And yet, even though she knew this attraction was highly inappropriate, it was also spectacularly thrilling.

She set the casserole dish on a mat on the table and lifted the lid.

Jack let out a soft groan. 'This is too good to be true.'

'What is?' She was tense as a violin string. The flash of heat in his eyes seemed to scorch her, but it disappeared as quickly as it had come, and he offered her a lopsided smile.

'Beauty, brains and a talent for cooking. You're quite a package, Senator Green.'

'Don't be too rash with the compliments until you've tasted the meal.'

Using a serving spoon, she lifted two ossobucci smothered in vegetable sauce onto Jack's plate. The smell was the same rich and appetising aroma she remembered from her grandmother's kitchen, and even though the meat probably wasn't young veal, it was tender and falling away from the bones, just as it should.

With a sense of relief Lizzie sat down to eat, but she couldn't completely relax until Jack had taken his first bite. To her dismay, he sat staring at his plate.

'Is something wrong, Jack?'

'No.' He picked up his knife and fork and sent her another crooked smile. 'I wondered where these bones had got to.'

'These bones?' she repeated in horrified alarm.

Jack grimaced, clearly embarrassed, and he shook his head. 'Don't worry. It's nothing. Shouldn't have mentioned it.' Immediately, he began to eat. 'Mmm. Lizzie, this is amazing.'

'But what were you saying about bones?' She couldn't eat until she knew.

'Don't worry about it. I shouldn't have said anything. Just relax and enjoy the meal. You've gone to a lot of trouble and it's sensational.'

'But I shouldn't have used these ossobucci, should I?'

Jack dropped his gaze to his plate. 'Well, I've never heard them called *that* before,' he admitted.

'What do you call them?'

His eyes were apologetic. 'Shin bones. We—er— usually keep them for the dogs.'

Caro Dio. Lizzie clasped a hand over her mouth. Tears stung her eyes.

'Lizzie.' Jack reached across the table and touched the back of her hand. 'It's OK. The meal's fabulous.'

'But you wanted the bones for your dogs.'

She sniffed. It would be ridiculous to cry.

'I didn't realise you could make a meal out of tough old bones, and, heaven knows, the dogs don't need them. Don't give it another thought.'

Jack's eyes sparkled at her, enticing from her an answering smile.

'I suppose it serves me right,' she admitted. 'I was trying too hard.' She gave a shaky laugh and a roll of her eyes. 'All those pots and pans.'

'This meal is worth every one of them,' Jack said, tucking in.

Lizzie ate, too, and she had to admit that the food tasted very good, but she could have saved herself an awful lot of work if she'd cooked something simple like spaghetti.

Why was it so hard for her to remember that she'd stepped out of the political circus ring? She didn't have to compete any more. She was here to relax. To slow down. Loosen up. Let go.

As they ate Jack encouraged her to talk, but, while most people expected her to talk about some aspect of her political work, he wanted to know more about her childhood in Italy, and she found herself unwinding as she recalled those happy times.

Many of her memories involved her little sisters, Jackie and Scarlett, and when she let her mind roll back she could almost hear the echoes of their laughter bouncing off their neighbours' houses as they chased each other down the cobbled streets. She could hear their girlish squeals as they ran up the hill, brushing past bushes of rosemary, catching its scent in their skirts, ducking beneath thorny branches in the lemon grove.

She told Jack about the sky in Monta Correnti, the unbelievable deep, deep blue of hyacinths, and the buttery sunlight that fell on ancient stone walls as she walked to school, clutching her mother's hand. She told him about the tangle of wild olive trees on the mountainside, the winding paths rimmed with autumn crocuses, her grandmother's cat asleep in the ivy.

Suddenly, she realised that Jack was staring at her, no longer easy-going, or relaxed, or smiling, but with an emotion that set her pulses racing.

'So beautiful,' he said softly.

Lizzie swallowed a gasp. She was almost certain he was talking about her, but this attraction thing was getting out of hand. She found it undeniably exciting, but it was wrong. Misplaced. She shouldn't allow Jack to speak to her like this.

'Yes, Italy's beautiful,' she said, pretending that she'd misunderstood him. 'But Australia's beautiful, too. Every country's beautiful in its own way.'

By now they'd finished their meal, and Lizzie stood to take their plates to the sink.

With a wry half-smile, Jack stood, too.

To her relief, he didn't try to repeat his compliment.

'Thank you,' he said instead. 'That was a memorable meal.'

'I'm glad you enjoyed it. I really liked your stroganoff last night.' Lizzie set the plates in the sink. 'I thought men were supposed to be messy cooks but you tossed that meal together so easily, *and* you only used one pot.'

From the sink, she threw a glance back over her shoulder to see Jack's reaction to this admission, was surprised to find him looking sheepish.

'Maybe that's because I only had to reheat the stroganoff,' he said.

Lizzie frowned. 'Excuse me?'

Standing there, with his hands shoved in his pockets, he looked like a little boy caught out for cheating in a spelling test. 'Bill, the cook, left the stroganoff in the freezer. I just had to heat it up.'

Lizzie's jaw dropped. 'But you let me think you'd made it from scratch.'

He shrugged. 'I didn't actually say I'd cooked it, but you seemed so impressed and I was happy to leave it that way.'

'Jack!' She couldn't believe he'd tricked her like that. How annoying.

Jack sent her a teasing smile. 'I should have known you'd turn the meals into a competition.'

'But I didn't!'

'Of course it was a competition, Lizzie.' Jack was moving towards her now. Laughter shimmered in his eyes as he came slowly, easily, across the kitchen, closer and closer. 'You can't help being competitive.' His voice was slow, deep, and teasing. 'Your mother named you after the Queen, and now you have to be top dog in everything.'

'That's not true.' As protests went, it was very weak. Lizzie threw up her hands in frustration.

Jack caught her wrists and held them fast.

Her breath was trapped in her throat. He was holding her by her wrists alone, and yet she felt pinned against the sink by the sheer force of his sexy masculinity. Looking up at him with a kind of fascinated awe, she could see that he wasn't smiling now.

She recognised the serious intent in his eyes. She'd seen it before, in other men, and she knew he wanted to kiss her. Oh, heavens, Jack was so very attractive and she could feel herself weakening, but she couldn't allow it. She was pregnant, for heaven's sake.

Their situation was precarious—a man and a woman alone in the middle of nowhere with a dangerously simmering attraction. Lizzie felt poised on a tightrope, about to fall, but she had to cling to common sense. She couldn't afford this kind of complication.

'Jack, you're invading my personal space.'

'Are you objecting?'

'Most definitely.' She spoke in her steeliest senatorial tones.

The light in Jack's eyes died. He let her wrists go and took a step back from her. For tense moments neither of them spoke, but they stared at each other, unhappily aware that a thrilling but reckless opportunity had been offered and rejected.

'So,' he said quietly, 'what would you like to do now?'

'I have to wash up.'

'You've washed up. It won't take a moment to throw these few things in the dishwasher. What then? Do you want to watch TV?' His mouth tilted in a half-mast smile. 'I'm assuming you'd like to keep up with the news.'

Lizzie imagined watching television with Jack, pictured him sprawled on the sofa, jeans stretched tight over solid, toned thighs. She knew she would spend the evening checking him out, and then he would know for sure how impossibly attracted she was.

She should keep her distance, calm down, get her head

straight. The news of the world would have to wait. She could always keep up with it via the Internet.

'No TV tonight, thanks,' she said as she headed for the door. 'I need to catch up on my emails.'

CHAPTER FOUR

SHE'D almost let Jack kiss her.

She'd *wanted* him to kiss her.

She'd very nearly jumped into his arms.

Lizzie stood at the doorway of her room, looking out across the front veranda to the quiet paddocks and the silvery trunks of gum trees, shocked by how close she'd come to wrecking her careful plans.

She'd come to Savannah to escape the pressures of the city, mostly to escape the pressure of journalists who'd just love to discover her pregnancy and turn it into a scandal. Yet tonight she'd been on the brink of creating a hot, new scandal.

With Jack.

She could imagine the headlines.

'Senator's Outback Love Nest.'

'Senator Takes a Cowboy.'

She'd wanted Jack to kiss her. Heaven help her, she'd practically *prayed* for amnesia. She'd wanted to forget her political responsibilities, and to forget she was forty and off men, and that she *always* picked the wrong men anyway. She'd wanted to forget that she was only here for a few short weeks, forget that her focus was on becoming a mother to an anonymous man's baby.

She'd wanted to forget everything...except the sexy sparkle in Jack's eyes and the alluring promise of his lips.

How scary it was to know she was so hopelessly weak. After years of self-discipline and hard work, after carefully weighing the pros and cons of single motherhood, tonight she'd wanted to risk it all while she carried on like a reckless, hormone-crazed kid.

Thank heavens nothing had happened.

She had to look on that encounter as a warning, and to be forewarned was to be forearmed. Now that she knew she was susceptible to Jack she would be much more careful in future.

On the back veranda, Jack stared out into the black night, idly stroking the springy fur between Cobber's ears while his mind replayed the scene in the kitchen.

He'd been so close to kissing Lizzie. Her mouth had been mere inches from his. He'd been able to smell her skin and the hint of lemony shampoo in her hair. He'd been about to taste her.

You're invading my personal space.

Are you objecting?

Most definitely.

'What do you reckon?' Jack asked the dog softly. 'Was that a stinging rejection? Or a lucky escape?'

Lizzie dreamed she was a child again. Wearing a blue dress and sandals, legs brown and bare, she wandered along the familiar, cobbled streets of Monta Correnti where purple petunias spilled from sunny balconies and washing hung from lines strung between windows.

Wherever she went, she could hear the church bell ringing the angelus from the top of the mountain, and she felt wonderfully safe.

But then, in the haphazard way that dreams changed, Lizzie was in her uncle Luca's kitchen where dried red peppers hung in loops from the ceiling and an old timber dresser held glassware and thick, blue and white plates. The fragrant aroma of tomato sauce, rich with basil and oregano, drifted from a pot on the stove.

Her cousins, Luca's twin boys, Alessandro and Angelo, were there in the dream, too. The three of them were eating spaghetti from deep bowls, slurping happily.

The scene changed again to a hot summer's night, and Lizzie and the twins were lying on the terrazzo balcony of her uncle's house, hoping for a cool breeze, while they looked up through stone arched windows to the jasmine-scented moon.

Suddenly, Isabella burst into the scene, but she was an adult, crying to Lizzie that she didn't know about the boys, and demanding to know where they'd come from.

When Lizzie woke the dream still felt real, even though Alessandro and Angelo had left Italy so very long ago— so long ago that Isabella and Lizzie's sisters hadn't even known about them.

Most of Lizzie's memories of the little boys were vague, but she could clearly remember their shiny eyes and cheeky smiles. She could definitely remember being in trouble with her mother for visiting Uncle Luca's house, and she remembered later being given strict orders never to speak to the rest of the family about the boys. Lizzie had never understood where they'd gone and she'd almost forgotten about them until her recent visit home.

With a heavy sigh, she rolled over in bed, cringing as she thought again about the terrible row that had erupted during her visit to Monta Correnti.

She'd gone to Italy full of her exciting baby news and she'd been even more excited about Isabella's engagement to Max, but she'd left hurt and bewildered, struggling to understand why her mother had so suddenly and angrily exposed the long-held secret that Luca had kept from his children.

Lisa was full of her own news because she'd just come back from New York where she'd seen a photo in the paper of Angelo, one of the twins who was a baseball star now. But... But it seemed incomprehensible to Lizzie that her mother would choose Luca's birthday to reveal the dark secret he'd kept from his children. Of course, the sudden news of the twins' existence had blown the family apart, but Isabella had been hit hardest of all.

But now that she was fully awake, Lizzie tried to shake off the dream. Last night, she'd reminded herself that she'd come to Savannah for a break, to focus on her pregnancy and on the changes that lay ahead. And yet here she was, still finding something to worry about.

By the time Lizzie arrived in the kitchen Jack had already breakfasted and gone, so she ate quickly, and returned to her room, carrying her mug of tea, where she downloaded her emails and discovered a brief message from her mother.

I'm too busy as always, but the restaurant is doing very well, so can't complain. I hope you're looking after yourself, darling. Do remember to take your iron tablets.

Lizzie knew she shouldn't have been surprised by the message's brevity. She should be used to her mother's ways by now.

Still, Lizzie longed to hear news of peace between her mother and her uncle. Perhaps it was too much to expect the brother and sister to kiss and make up. Just the same, she was worried. And there was still no message from Isabella. She'd sent her cousin several emails now, but Isabella was yet to reply.

There was every chance, of course, that Isabella was extremely busy. She'd always worked harder than anyone else, taking care of her smaller brothers after their mother died. Even now, when she was engaged to a wealthy Italian prince, Isabella was still working hard in the family restaurant.

Given Isabella's devotion to her family, it was no wonder she'd been especially upset by the news of Alessandro and Angelo in America. And it was completely understandable that she'd resented the fact that Lizzie had known about her brothers all along.

Thinking about it now, Lizzie felt as if she were almost as guilty as her mother was, which was pretty silly. She'd been a child, after all, and she'd promised to keep the secret without understanding any of it.

A sudden knock on Lizzie's door interrupted her thoughts. She whirled around, saw Jack standing there, sunburned and smiling in his dusty work clothes, and she was overcome by another astonishing burst of pleasure, as if someone had lit a flame inside her.

'How are you?' he asked.

'Fine, thanks.' Was she grinning foolishly?

'I was wondering if you're madly busy.'

Normally she would have responded automatically that of course she was terribly busy, but this morning she recognised how much like her mother that sounded.

'Why do you ask?'

'I was hoping you could lend me a hand again. Another quick job. I need to get feed to the newly weaned calves, the ones not included in the muster.'

To Lizzie's dismay, his request had instant appeal. She

told herself it was because she felt motherly towards the weaned calves. 'What does it involve?'

'I was hoping you could drive the truck. It's only a matter of driving slowly along a track, and I'd be on the back pushing off bales of stock feed.'

'I've never driven a truck.'

'It's a standard floor gear shift.' Jack grinned. 'And it's perfectly harmless now.'

Her first thought was for her baby's safety, but she was sure Jack wouldn't put her in a dangerous vehicle. Then she thought about how slow this job would be for him if he had to do it on his own—stopping the truck, leaping out and climbing onto the back to push off a bale or two, then jumping down and driving on to repeat the job, over and over. 'When do you want to do this?'

'Late this afternoon? Say, about four o'clock?'

She refused to smile. 'All right.'

For the rest of the day, an uncalled-for tingle of excitement zipped through Lizzie every time she thought about her late-afternoon assignment with Jack. *It's only work. It's perfectly harmless.*

She worked steadily, lunching on a sandwich at her desk, but promptly at four o'clock, dressed in blue jeans and a long-sleeved, blue and white striped cotton shirt, which she'd jokingly thought of as her country-woman shirt, she met Jack outside the machinery shed.

The sun was already slipping to the west and it sent a pretty, coppery-tinged light over the bales of hay on the back of the truck. Feeling only a little nervous, Lizzie climbed behind the driver's wheel for a practice drive, while Jack swung into the passenger seat beside her.

To her relief, the truck's motor started first go, and when

she eased the vehicle forward there was only one kangaroo-hop and one teeth-clenching clash of gears before she got the hang of it and drove smoothly. Jack pointed the way via a dirt track that wound through paddocks of dry grass dotted with gum trees, and Lizzie drove on, appreciative of the quietness of the outback afternoon—the wide starch blue skies, the distant mauve hills and white-trunked gums, all bathed in soft, golden light.

It was such a very different world out here.

Having grown up in Italy, Lizzie still found herself marvelling at the sheer size of Australian properties. Savannah station was miles from Gidgee Springs, the nearest township, and it was a thousand miles from Brisbane, thousands more from Sydney, from Canberra and Melbourne.

Every so often they came to a gate, and this time it was Jack who got out to open them, and then close them behind her, but it wasn't too long before they reached the huge paddock with the weaned calves.

'OK. This is where I start dropping off the feed,' Jack said. 'All you have to do is drive on slowly and we'll drop a line of feed across a couple of kilometres.'

Using the rear-vision mirrors as guides, Lizzie watched him swing up onto the tray-back of the truck with his customary ease. She drove slowly, watching him framed in the mirror, with his shirtsleeves rolled back over muscled forearms, using his pocket knife to cut the twine on the big bales of hay, then tossing them to the ground, as if they weighed no more than sugar cubes.

Young cattle came from everywhere, head butting each other like schoolboys tussling in a tuck-shop queue in their eagerness to get at the fresh sweet hay.

Too soon all the hay was dispersed and Lizzie stopped

the truck, while Jack dismounted and got back in beside her. 'Well done,' he said with a smile. 'I'll make a country-woman of you before you're through.'

They exchanged smiling glances.

Jack said, 'You'll be riding a horse next.'

'Oh, no, I won't.' No way would she threaten her pregnancy on the back of a horse.

Again, she considered telling Jack about her baby. After all, he was very friendly, and he'd managed to thaw her frostiness despite her best efforts to remain remote.

Perhaps she might have told him if she was confident that he wanted no more than friendship, but she couldn't ignore last night's close call, and the inappropriate, two-way attraction that seemed to be getting stronger every minute. There was enough tension beween them already without adding her pregnancy to the mix.

When they reached the homestead and climbed down from the truck, Jack was surprised that Lizzie didn't seem in any hurry to go back inside. Instead, she walked to the timber fence of the stockyard and leaned her elbows on the top rail, looking out across the plains.

The sun was low in the west now, tingeing the sky with pink, and a cool breeze stirred the grasses. Lizzie, in her blue jeans and striped shirt, looked amazingly at home in that setting. Her profile, softened by loosened strands of dark hair, was pensive as she looked out at the land.

Jack couldn't resist going over to her. 'A penny for your thoughts.'

'I was thinking how very peaceful it is here.' She lifted her face to the rosy sky and took a deep breath. 'Especially now, at this time of day. The light's so soft and the land's all lovely and dappled by shadows.'

'If you can't relax here, you never will.'

She sent him a rueful smile. 'Is it living here that makes you so relaxed? Is everyone in the outback easy-going?'

'Not everyone. My father certainly wasn't.'

'I've been wondering about your family,' she said. 'Are they still on the land?'

'No.' Jack's shoulders slumped and he leaned heavily on the rail beside her. 'I'm an only child and my parents split up years ago. Mum went to Melbourne to live with her sister, and my father died of a heart attack about six months later.'

'I'm sorry.'

Jack gave a dismissive shrug. 'Mum's remarried now, and very happy.'

'And you stayed on the land, working for Kate?'

The breeze caught a strand of Lizzie's hair, blowing it towards Jack. He contemplated catching it, letting it slide through his fingers like a satin ribbon, then he came to his senses and erased the thought, answered her question instead.

'I ended up here eventually, but it wasn't what I'd planned for my life.' He dragged his gaze from Lizzie and watched a bird circling high above them. 'My parents used to own a cattle property almost as big as Savannah.'

Lizzie turned to him, her face soft with sympathy. 'Is it too nosy to ask what happened?'

'We lost it thanks to my pig-headed father.' Jack grimaced. 'My old man argued with everyone—the local council, auctioneers, neighbours, bank managers. He completely ignored his accountant's advice, made a stack of rash investments on the stock exchange, and lost all his money. The bank tried to foreclose on the property, and Dad had a whale of a time, arguing and resisting.'

'Did they take him to court?'

Jack nodded. 'The trial dragged on for ages, but the old

man wouldn't compromise and settle out of court. He wanted a fight. Stubborn as a broken bulldozer. In the end—' he gave a shrug '—we lost the lot.'

'Ouch,' Lizzie said softly. 'That must have been terribly hard for you and your mother.'

'It was the last straw. Ended their marriage.' Jack's mouth thinned. 'Dad died six months later, still furious with the world and everyone in it.'

It was a terrible story.

Lizzie almost wished she hadn't asked. Jack's eyes had completely lost their usual sparkle and they'd taken on a haunted look, as if he was seeing ghosts that still troubled him.

Surely it was a miracle he'd come through such an unhappy time without losing his cheerful and easy-going temperament. She wondered how much it had cost him to retain the 'Jack-factor' that she'd taken for granted.

'At least you know you're not anything like your father, Jack.'

'I should bloody well hope not. I've gone out of my way to make sure I'm not even remotely like him.'

'So you ended up working for Kate instead,' Lizzie said to change the subject.

'I got involved with Savannah after Kate's husband died, and she had all sorts of trouble. Corporate cowboys tried to frighten her into selling this place for a pittance.'

'But you were able to help her?'

'I had to,' he said with an offhand shrug. 'Kate might be a tough old cookie, but at that time she was a grieving widow and she couldn't stand up to those thugs on her own.'

So, Lizzie thought as darkness crept over Savannah and they left the stockyard and headed for the house, Jack had deliberately chosen to be different from his dad. Mr Nice

Guy. But although he was easy-going, he wasn't a push-over. He'd proved that when he'd stood up for Kate.

Even so, Jack had chosen well to stay here in the out-back where the only stress came from the weather and the seasons and the market fluctuations.

The lifestyle here suited him. He would hate her frantic pace, and for the thousandth time Lizzie told herself she was pleased she'd called a halt to last night's kiss.

The little niggle of regret that squirmed in her chest would disappear in time. Surely?

'You can cook a mean steak,' she declared at dinner.

Jack sent her one of his trademark smiles. 'Just as well you like it. I don't have a very wide repertoire.'

'Doesn't matter. This will do me.'

The steak was cooked to perfection, blackened and seared on the outside and rosy pink in the middle, and the accompanying lettuce, tomatoes and radishes were wonderfully crisp, straight from the garden.

They didn't talk a great deal as they ate. Lizzie wondered if Jack regretted having shared so much about his family. He didn't seem particularly upset, but perhaps he was good at hiding his feelings beneath his easy-going exterior.

Or perhaps she was thinking about him far too much.

'Would you like ice cream for dessert?' he asked as he cleared their dishes.

'Oh, no dessert for me.' Lizzie patted her stomach, aware of the bulge below her navel that seemed to be grow-ing exponentially.

'It's chocolate-fudge ripple.' Jack sent her a cheeky wink as he opened the freezer door.

Her taste buds leapt. 'No, I really shouldn't.'

He shrugged. 'Your loss.'

Didn't he worry about triglycerides? She supposed he could offset his eating habits with plenty of outdoor exercise.

Watching Jack fill a bowl with rich creamy scoops of vanilla and chocolate, she folded her arms and resisted the temptation to lick her lips. To her surprise, when he sat down again he handed her a spoon.

'In case you change your mind.' A slow smile unravelled, lighting his green eyes. 'I'm happy to share.'

Share?

Lizzie flashed back to her student days with Mitch and the way he'd so easily charmed and enslaved her. She'd made more mistakes over guys since then, especially with Toby. Hadn't she finally learned her lesson? Shouldn't she reject such easy familiarity from Jack?

But she was ridiculously relieved to see him looking happy again, and, after all, what was the harm in a spoonful of dessert? Lizzie lasted almost no time— perhaps, oh, all of twenty seconds—before she reached across the table and took a spoonful of ice cream from Jack's bowl.

It was cool and creamy against her tongue and it tasted sinfully luscious.

'Good, isn't it?' Jack said, pushing the bowl closer.

'Mmm.' She helped herself to a second spoonful.

'Not quite as good as Italian gelato, I guess.'

'Oh, I think this ice cream could hold its own.'

Jack grinned. 'So you don't feel compelled to stick up for everything Italian?'

'Why should I? I'm half Australian. My father's Australian.'

'I guessed with a surname like Green that he wasn't Italian. Does he live in Australia or Italy?'

'In Australia. In Sydney.'

Jack looked as if he wanted to ask another question, but was holding back.

It seemed only fair to expand her story, after he'd told her so much about his family. 'My mother was a fashion model,' she said. 'She travelled a lot when she was young, and she met my father when he was a dive master at a resort on the Great Barrier Reef.

'And no,' Lizzie added, guessing the direction of Jack's thoughts. 'My parents didn't marry. My father stayed here in Australia and my mother went back to Italy. I lived with her, mostly in Monta Correnti, until I started university. By then, my father had a boat-building business in Sydney, and I wanted to study English literature, so I decided to come out here to study, to be near him and to get to know his family and his country.'

'He must have been pleased about that.'

'Yes, he was. Very pleased.' Lizzie smiled, remembering their wonderful, emotion-filled meeting. It had been such a shock to discover how very deeply her father loved her, and how much he'd missed her.

Jack was watching her closely. 'And you've stayed on,' he said, 'so you must have liked it here.'

'Yes,' she said simply.

She helped herself to one last spoonful of ice cream, tipping her head back and holding the icy sweetness in her mouth until it began to melt, slipping slowly, languorously down her throat.

Out of the corner of her eye she caught Jack staring at her, and the unmistakable desire in his eyes sent flames shooting under her skin. Ribbons of heat formed knots in the pit of her stomach.

Caro Dio. She reached for her glass of mineral water

and took a deep swig, and then another, draining it. 'I—
I'll do the dishes,' she muttered, jumping to her feet.

Slowly, Jack scooped the last of the ice cream from the
bowl and then even more slowly he licked the spoon. When
he stood, at last, and came lazily towards her, she realised
she hadn't done a thing about the dishes. She was still
standing there, watching him.

He set the bowl on the sink and his arm brushed hers.
Another flash of heat engulfed her. He didn't move away.

It was a breathless age before he said in a low, lazy
drawl, 'I'm invading your personal space.'

'Yes.'

It was no more than a whisper. Tonight she couldn't
dredge up the right level of frostiness.

Jack placed a hand on the bench on either side of her,
trapping her against the cupboards. 'I'd like to stay here,
Lizzie.'

No. No. No. No. No. This was where she had to tell Jack,
again, to step back, to stop saying such things.

She tried to speak. Couldn't summon the words. Heaven
help her, she was too enchanted by the gathering storm
inside her, and, already, she could feel the heat of his body
surrounding her.

Already he was touching her. His hands slid lightly up
her arms. She was shivering. Melting. His arms were closing
around her...while his lips explored the curve of her neck.

She closed her eyes, savouring the astonishing, sweet
pressure of Jack's mouth on her skin.

There was no way she could stop him. It had been so
long since she'd experienced this gentle intimacy. Too
long. She could feel her skin smiling wherever his lips
touched her.

Her skin grew greedy and she arched her neck, seeking

more. Jack obliged beautifully, letting warm, lazy kisses trail over her neck to her jaw, while his hands traced the shape of her shoulders through the thin fabric of her T-shirt.

At any moment now their mouths would touch, and all chance of stopping him would fly out of the window.

It was already too late.

She was filled with a sweet, aching need that deadened all thoughts but her deepening yearning to be touched and kissed… She was desperate for the moment when Jack's mouth finally reached hers…

When it happened, her lips were already parted.

Breathlessly, he whispered her name. 'Lizzie.' Just once, brushing the soft syllables over her open lips. Then his tongue traced the rim of her parted mouth, and her knees turned to water.

Jack caught her, and she was instantly lost, drowning in the perfect taste and smell of him, in the hint of sun-drenched outdoors that clung to his skin.

Everything about his kiss was perfect—the texture of his mouth, and his grainy skin, and the muscly strength of his body pressing against her.

She felt rosy and warm and insanely happy.

When Jack broke the kiss, she was devastated. She'd wanted it to go on for ever.

Clearly, Jack had much more control than she had. With one last gentle kiss on her forehead, he released her.

He smiled. 'You taste delicious. Of ice cream.'

'So do you.'

She was smiling goofily when, without warning, common sense returned like a cold slap. What on earth was she doing? How could she have been such a fool? The kiss was a mistake, and the way she'd responded was an even bigger mistake.

Jack would think she was available for further seduction. She wasn't available. She was here for a brief stay. She was years older than he was, and she was pregnant, while he was young and fit and virile.

'We shouldn't have let that happen,' she said.

Jack smiled easily. 'Of course we should.'

'But—' Her mind skidded and slipped as she tried to think sensibly. She couldn't start a relationship with this cowboy. The press would have a field day.

With an air of desperation, she said, 'We hardly know each other.'

Jack stared at her for long, thoughtful seconds. 'I suppose I should have asked if there's a man in your life.'

'Yes, you should have.' Lizzie knew she had to take control. 'We need to talk about this, Jack. To set some ground rules.'

When he didn't object she was relieved that he was being reasonable. Now that they'd broken the spell, she couldn't believe she'd let things get so out of hand without asking all kinds of questions. The kinds of questions nearly every sane man or woman asked before leaping into each other's arms.

But the questions were also the sort that would lead to informing Jack that she was pregnant, and already she could picture him reeling back with shocked dismay, could feel the chill of isolation as he retreated from her.

She knew it was appallingly wrong of her, but in that moment she wished they'd both stayed crazy for just a little longer.

CHAPTER FIVE

THEY went through to the lounge room.

To talk.

Jack still couldn't believe he was doing this, couldn't believe he'd pulled back from the most sensational kiss he'd ever known. He'd been a lost man, on the very brink of taking an Australian federal senator. Right there. In the kitchen.

Unless he was terribly mistaken, she'd been as swept away as he was. In another five seconds they might have been too lost in passion to stop.

Now, it was hard to be grateful for the inner voice that had urged him to remember why Kate Burton had sent Lizzie Green to Savannah.

She'd wanted Lizzie to be safe. Safe. In his care. She was in some kind of trouble and she'd been placed under his protection. He knew zero about her private life. Which meant he had no choice but to cool his heels, and his ardour, until he'd extracted satisfactory answers.

So, yeah. He'd let Lizzie talk, and he'd listen, and *then* he'd kiss her senseless.

As Lizzie took a seat in Jack's lounge room, she was sure she'd never felt more shaken or self-conscious. She was, of course, grateful for this reprieve. If she hadn't stopped Jack, she would have broken every single one of her relationship rules. But she felt bereft now, rather than thankful.

She also felt terribly exposed.

From the moment she'd decided to be a single mum, she'd been so careful to hold men at bay. Relationships simply weren't worth the pain.

Tonight, Jack Lewis had ripped through her defences. From the very first touch of his lips she'd been shameless, and even though she'd stopped him, she was certain he knew *exactly* how needy she was. Even though she was sitting primly with her ankles crossed, he could probably guess that he only had to reach out and touch her and she'd be scrambling down the sofa and into his arms.

Oh, for heaven's sake, get rid of those thoughts. Get over it.

At least Jack didn't ply her with questions the minute they were seated. Lizzie didn't want to discuss the men or lack of men in her life and she was grateful for the chance to sit in the lamplight, nursing a mug of peppermint tea while she gathered her wits. She had to work out how to warn Jack off, and, as they were still going to be living together, it had to be done nicely.

A practised tactician, she took the roundabout route. 'The silence out here is really quite amazing,' she said. 'I found it strange at first. In my apartment in Brisbane there's constant background noise—traffic, building construction, roadwork. Sirens blaring day and night.'

'I suppose you get used to the noise and you don't even hear it after a while.'

'That's true.' Lizzie turned to Jack. 'Have you spent much time in the city?'

He answered with a shake of his head, then he smiled.

'But I do enjoy the big smoke, and when I get there I make the most of it.'

'I suppose you paint the town red?'

His smile took a wicked tilt. 'Wouldn't you like to know?'

Actually, yes, Lizzie thought, dismayed. She was unbearably curious about the fun Jack got up to in the city, but no way would she admit it.

Jack looked annoyingly at ease now, sprawled casually at his end of the sofa, long legs loose and relaxed, his body angled Lizzie's way.

He was even able to smile. 'OK. You were going to tell me about the men in your life. Where would you like to start?'

'Actually, I don't think we should even begin, Jack. We should just accept that the kiss was a mistake and—'

'That's rubbish, Lizzie, and you know it.'

'What do you mean?'

'The kiss was fantastic and we're going to do it again.' Jack's eyes flashed emerald fire. 'Unless you have a damn good reason why we shouldn't.'

Lizzie looked away, afraid that she might blush.

'For example,' Jack said, 'it would be helpful to know if there's a boyfriend back in Canberra, or Brisbane, or wherever.'

After too long, she admitted softly, 'There's no one.'

'You're sure?'

'Of course I'm sure. It's not the kind of thing I'd forget. I—I haven't been in a relationship for some time.'

Surely Jack didn't need to know about Mitch, the first man who'd broken her heart, or about Toby, her banker lover who'd leaked their story to the press and almost finished her career?

She shot Jack a sharp glance. 'The question works both ways, Jack. What about you? Do you have a girlfriend?'

She held her breath, realising that she was far too interested in his answer.

'There's no one with a claim on me,' he said quietly.

It wasn't quite the unambiguous answer she would have preferred.

After a small silence, he said, 'So if there's no man in your life, what's the problem, Lizzie?'

She hesitated. After kissing him into oblivion, it wasn't going to be easy to explain that she didn't want a relationship.

'You've come here to get away from something, haven't you?' he said.

'Well, yes,' she admitted, grateful for the lead. 'Mostly, I wanted to keep away from journalists.'

'Any special reason? I thought politicians thrived on publicity.'

Of course there was a special reason, but Lizzie still baulked at telling Jack about her baby. She tried to picture sharing her news, going through the involved explanation and her reasons for choosing the sperm-donor option.

She had no idea how Jack would react. For some people, the whole idea of a single woman choosing an anonymous donor was too new, too confronting. Telling anyone about her pregnancy was like letting a genie out of a bottle. She never knew what kind of reaction she would get, but once it was out, it was impossible to cram it back. The damage was done.

Instead, she said, 'Unfortunately, journalists always target female politicians.'

'Especially the photogenic ones,' Jack suggested dryly.

Lizzie nodded. 'I'm afraid I've been called a bimbo once too often. It's beyond annoying. It doesn't matter how hard, or how seriously I take my job, journalists take one look at me and decide my head's full of chiffon and sequins.'

He smiled in sympathy. 'So how did you get into politics

in the first place? Was it really like you said? Something you sort of fell into?'

'Well…yes. It was…more or less.'

'Like Alice down the rabbit hole?'

She couldn't help smiling. 'Some people do say the PM looks like the Cheshire cat, but my story isn't nearly as interesting as Alice's.'

'I'm interested.' Jack's eyes burned, as if challenging her.

Lizzie squirmed. Any explanation would involve talking about Mitch. Then again, if Jack understood more about her, he might keep his distance.

'I think it started when I was very young,' she said. 'Way back when I was at school in Monta Correnti. My best friend's father was the mayor, and I used to go and play at Gianna's house. Her father wasn't home very often, but when he was, he was always kind and so much fun. Never too busy to talk to us.'

Dipping her head, Lizzie breathed in the scent of her peppermint tea. 'And I'd always hear grown-ups saying how wonderful Gianna's father was because he fixed our town's water and sewers, and helped the old people. The whole town loved him. I think he was probably my first inspiration.'

'But you chose Australian politics,' Jack said.

'Yes. When I started at Sydney uni, I was excited to discover how certain movements and certain ways of thinking could positively affect the world. I was full of noble aims—wanting to help people, to make the world a better place, to represent neglected viewpoints.'

She gave a self-conscious laugh. 'Then I fell madly in love with a politician.'

The mild amusement in Jack's eyes vanished. 'Who was he?'

Lizzie took another sip of tea. 'Have you heard of Mitchell MacCallum?'

'Of course.' Jack looked distinctly shocked. 'Don't tell me he was the one?'

Lizzie nodded. Even now, after all this time, saying Mitch's name out loud sent a chill chasing down her spine.

An awkward silence fell over the room, and Jack sat very still, frowning. She could almost see his mind working, thinking back through everything he'd heard and read about Mitchell MacCullum.

'This was well before the scandal,' she said.

'I should hope so,' he replied grimly.

So Jack had a very low opinion of Mitch. Lizzie wasn't surprised. Five years ago, the media had left little room for sympathy when they had exposed Mitch. He'd been married for years by then, and he'd been caught using his ministerial expense account to keep a mistress in a penthouse on Sydney Harbour.

Jack said tightly, 'Tell me more about MacCallum.'

She hesitated, but now that she'd started she might as well get it over with, so she took a deep breath and dived in. 'Mitch and I were both at Sydney University. Actually, we were housemates. There were five of us, sharing a big, old, tumbledown house in Balmain. He was a couple of years ahead of me, studying political science and economics. He was brilliant and charismatic, and I suppose you could say I became a kind of disciple.'

'A disciple who slept with the prophet.'

'Eventually.' A hot blush burned her cheeks. 'At first I simply spent hours in the university refectory, or in coffee bars listening to Mitch talk. He was incredibly articulate about human rights and international relations, and he championed all kinds of student causes. He was head of the student union, and a wonderful debater, so he was very easy to listen to.'

Jack looked as if he was going to say something, but changed his mind. He simply offered a thoughtful nod, like a journalist in a TV interview, and waited for her to continue with her story.

'After that, I started going to political rallies with Mitch. It all seemed very intellectual and idealistic and exciting, and when he graduated and decided to stand for parliament, I joined his campaign team. I spent every spare moment painting banners and putting up posters, doing clerical work, and running errands.'

'I dare say MacCallum was incredibly appreciative of your efforts.'

The hard glitter in Jack's eyes surprised Lizzie. Clearly, he disliked Mitch intensely.

'So what happened after he was elected?'

'I was given a job on his staff,' she said quietly.

'I'm sure you'd earned it.'

Jack wasn't referring to her help with the campaign, but Lizzie ignored the dig. 'We were working on really interesting and worthwhile programmes, and Mitch was invited to all kinds of receptions and charity balls. I'd never had such a busy social life.'

'And I suppose you'd moved out of the student share house by this time.'

'Yes.' Lizzie took a sip of her cooling tea as she remembered the day she and Mitch had moved into their own apartment. She'd been so thrilled. It had felt like a public announcement that she was Mitchell MacCallum's girlfriend.

Of course, she'd been desperately in love, and she'd expected that Mitch would propose to her at any moment, but there was no way she would share that dream with Jack.

She said, simply, 'I lived with him for about three months, and then—' she straightened her shoulders, determined not to let Jack see that any of this bothered her after all this time '—Mitch's party leaders decided that he needed a more settled image. They wanted him to marry.'

Jack frowned. 'So? Why didn't *you* marry him?'

'I wasn't given the opportunity.' She forced an extra-bright smile. 'Mitch married Amanda Leigh, the daughter of a former state governor. She came from one of Melbourne's most influential families, you see, so she had fabulous links to the old-school-tie network.'

'So, MacCallum showed his true colours.' Again, Jack spoke with clear distaste.

But then all the hardness fell out of his face. 'Lizzie,' he said, watching her intently. 'I can't believe you let him treat you like that.'

'It wasn't a matter of letting him. He did it on the sly. I went home to Italy to spend Christmas with my family and by the time I got back it was a *fait accompli*. My supposed boyfriend was married. He laughed it off, said we both knew there wasn't a future for us. But, of course, I'd had this silly idea—'

She bit down hard on her lip to stop herself from giving way to self-pity. 'Anyway,' she said quickly. 'I've gone off track. I was supposed to be telling you how I ended up in the senate.'

Her tea was stone cold by now, but she downed the last of it and set the mug on the coffee table. 'I resigned from Mitch's staff. I couldn't stay there—it would have been too awkward. But the party hierarchy didn't want to lose a hard worker. There was a vacancy on the senate ticket and they wanted a youthful candidate, preferably female.'

Lizzie shrugged. 'It was time to stop feeling sorry for

myself, and I could see this was a chance to do something to help others, so I said I'd give it a go. And I found myself elected.'

'And you've been there ever since.'

'It becomes a way of life.'

Jack was frowning again. 'What does that mean? Are you planning to stay there for ever?'

'The voters may not want me there for ever.' She forced a laugh. 'I certainly don't want to be an old lady senator.'

Ever since he'd started talking about the future, a worried shadow had lingered in Jack's eyes. Lizzie wondered what was bothering him. She thought about his kiss, and could still feel the tummy-tingling pleasure of his lips on her skin, the tantalising intimacy of his tongue. His thrilling mix of fire and tenderness.

It was a shock to realise that in a matter of days he'd penetrated the tough outer armour she'd spent so long building. For a brief moment, he'd exposed her softer centre. But surely he understood their kiss couldn't lead to anything serious?

She should make that clear. Now.

Before she could speak, however, Jack rose. 'You're looking pale and tired.'

Lizzie wasn't surprised. She felt emotionally drained and physically exhausted.

'You'd better get to bed.' To her surprise, Jack came towards her, bent low and kissed her cheek, just as a brother might. 'Goodnight.'

Puzzled, she watched him leave the room.

When they'd started this conversation, Jack had shown every intention of taking up where their passionate kiss had left off, but she'd achieved her goal. Her story about Mitch had been enough to make him think twice.

She knew she should be pleased and relieved. By walking away from their situation, Jack had saved her the trouble of explaining about the baby.

To Lizzie's annoyance, she couldn't feel grateful. She felt confused. And just a little sad.

She went back to her room and tried to read, but thoughts of Jack kept intruding, shattering her concentration.

The kiss loomed large, of course, and each time she struggled to fight off the memories.

She was off men. She was only here for a short time, focusing on being a mum. The last thing she'd expected or needed was a potential boyfriend in the outback.

It was all rather distressing. To centre herself once more, she leafed through her favourite book about single pregnancy, about mothers who'd met and conquered the challenges of raising their babies on their own. She lingered over the beautiful photos—even the first startling photo of an attractive blonde lawyer giving birth.

Lizzie viewed childbirth with a mixture of fascination, incredulity and awe. Right now, it was still hard to believe that it was actually going to happen to her.

She moved quickly on to other, more reassuring pictures— a mother breastfeeding her baby, another woman laughing as she bathed a chubby baby boy. There was a mother sitting cross-legged on the lounge-room floor, playing with blocks with her curly-headed toddler. Another mother pushed a pram through a park strewn with autumn leaves.

The very last photo was of a single mum with twins.

Twins. Now that was a scary thought. Lizzie always skipped quickly past this page. There were twins in her family, but she couldn't possibly imagine being the mother of twins. It would be too difficult to juggle a career and two babies without the support of a partner.

She lay awake for hours trying not to worry about that.

* * *

Jack rose at dawn and went straight to the horse paddock. Within minutes, he was mounted on Archer, a long-legged grey, and together they took off at a thundering gallop across the mist-wreathed plains.

It was good to be outdoors at this early hour. Archer was sure-footed, the autumn morning was cool and crisp, and heavy dew had dampened the earth, so the dust was at a minimum.

From as far back as he could remember Jack had loved riding, and, with any luck, this morning's long, hard gallop would knock the tension out of his muscles, and provide him with the necessary space and distance to think with a clear head.

He had to decide how he was going to handle the crazy situation he found himself in now—infatuated, after just one kiss, with a woman who couldn't be more wrong for him.

When Lizzie arrived in the kitchen for breakfast, her first surprise was a cleared table. All the mess was gone and instead there was a second surprise. A note propped against the teapot.

> *I've gone for a ride, so don't wait for me. Help*
> *yourself to breakfast. I'll catch you later.*
> *Jack.*

Her first reaction was disappointment. She'd spent far too much time last night trying to stop thinking about him. She'd come to breakfast, not sure what to expect, but determined to put last night's kiss out of her thoughts and to carry on as if it hadn't happened. Nevertheless, she'd been filled with fluttery anticipation.

It was silly, but she'd actually been wondering if he might have another job for her. She'd even practised asking super-casually… *I don't suppose you need a hand today, Jack? Sing out, if there's any odd job you need help with.*

The fact that Jack was probably avoiding her bothered her more than it should.

As she made herself a cup of tea, a boiled egg and toast she wondered if she'd totally annoyed him by responding to his kiss so eagerly and then claiming it was a mistake. It was the kind of nonsense you'd expect from a teenager. At forty, she was supposed to know better.

Problem was, when Jack was around, Lizzie felt closer to fourteen than forty.

At the edge of the plain, Jack reined Archer to a halt, and walked the grey closer to the overhang of the rugged red cliff. From there he could see the river in the gorge far below, snaking over its bed of sand.

Dismounting, he wrapped the reins around a gidgee sapling and hunkered on the red earth, watching the sunlight hit the river and turn it to silver…

He drank in the silence, let it seep into him. Then, like a dog digging up a favourite, well-gnawed bone, he let his mind tussle with his problem.

The lady senator.

Just thinking about her made his body tighten. Remembering the way she'd kissed and the way her curvy body had melted beneath his hands only made matters worse. He wanted her so badly.

And he knew she'd been turned on, too.

OK, she'd called a halt, and she'd spent half an hour telling him about that rat MacCallum who'd hurt her, but

Jack had seen the flare of disappointment in her eyes when he'd left her last night.

They were both trying to fight their chemistry. The tension was crazy. Being in a room together was a new form of torture, but what was he going to do about it?

He tried to tick off all the reasons he should stay clear of Lizzie Green. The first was obvious—she was a city-based career woman, and a federal politician, a woman with plenty of power and very big goals, and why would he get involved with someone like that when he'd finally thrown off the shadow of his pushy, overreaching father?

His next reason for avoiding Lizzie was shakier. She was quite a bit older than him, but for the life of him Jack couldn't turn that into a problem. Lizzie's age made her earthier and more womanly than any of the sweet young things he'd dated in the last few years.

It wasn't as if he were planning to marry Lizzie or anything…

Damn. He'd ridden out here to gain clarity, but the ride wasn't much help.

He'd already run out of objections…

The lady senator was worth another try.

Lizzie was finishing her breakfast when it occurred to her that Jack's absence provided a golden opportunity to phone Kate Burton. She didn't want to pry behind Jack's back, but she could ask pertinent questions about him that she should have raised before she'd left for Savannah.

To her dismay, Kate laughed at her very first question. 'You'd like to know more about Jack? Lizzie, my dear girl, that's delightful news.'

'I should think it's only common sense,' Lizzie said

defensively. 'After all, I'm living alone with him for weeks on end.'

'Of course.' Kate still sounded amused, but then she sobered. 'Jack hasn't given you any—how shall I put it?— any cause for concern, has he?'

'Oh, no, not at all. He's been a perfect gentleman— perfect *host*,' she amended quickly. 'He's rather younger than I expected.'

Kate laughed again. 'Oh, Jack's at least thirty, I'm sure.'

Ten years younger than me. Lizzie wished she didn't feel so disheartened by this news. Why was it relevant?

'You might have warned me that he would be the only other person here,' Lizzie said.

'Is he?' Kate sounded surprised. 'Where are the cook and the ringers?'

'Out on a cattle muster, apparently.'

'Oh, dear,' Kate said. 'So who's cooking?'

'Jack and I. But that's not a problem. We're taking it in turns.'

'Lovely.' Kate very quickly brightened again. 'I'm not sure about Jack's cooking ability, but at least he's good company, and he's as handsome as the devil. You must agree that's a definite plus, Lizzie.'

'Well—I—maybe.'

'Don't worry, Lizzie. Jack might look like a larrikin, but his heart's in the right place.'

'I imagine he's been quite helpful to you?'

'Absolutely. When my Arthur died, I had all sorts of trouble. People were trying to frighten me into selling Savannah for much less than it's worth. Jack stepped in and rescued me. It was just wonderful to see the way he stood up to those fellows.'

'Thank heavens he did.'

'Yes, Jack's a darling, and he's totally trustworthy. I wouldn't have sent you to Savannah if he wasn't.'

'Oh, I didn't doubt that.' The word *trustworthy* settled inside Lizzie. Given her disastrous history with men, it gave out a warm little glow. 'Thank you for reassuring me. I'm surprised Jack didn't—'

Lizzie broke off in mid-sentence, suddenly distracted by the sight, through the window, of a horse and rider galloping towards the homestead.

The rider had to be Jack, but he seemed to be approaching at a breakneck speed, heading straight for the stockyard fence, and it was a tall fence, made of solid timber rails.

Lizzie gasped. Surely the fence was too high. Jack couldn't possibly clear it.

'Lizzie, are you there?'

'Yes, Kate. I—um—just a moment.'

Another gasp broke from her as Jack and his horse thundered closer.

Why wasn't he slowing down? Lizzie was already flinching, sure there was going to be a horrible crash.

Horrified, she held her breath as Jack's figure crouched low in the saddle while the magnificent grey horse gathered its long legs beneath it.

'Lizzie!' Kate cried. 'Speak to me. What's going on there?'

In the next instant Jack's horse took off in a magnificent leap, sailing over the fence and clearing it easily, landing in the home paddock as neatly as a ballet dancer.

Lizzie let out a whoosh of breath, and realised she was shaking. 'I—I'm sorry, Kate. It's just that Jack took his horse over this terribly high fence and I didn't think he could possibly make it.'

'Not the stockyard gate?'

'Yes. How did you know?'

'Good heavens. Is he all right?'

'Yes,' Lizzie said again and she was grinning now. 'He's fine. Absolutely fine.'

Kate let out a surprising whoop of delight. 'Lizzie, that's amazing.'

'Is it?'

'Yes. Good heavens, dear, Jack's just done something quite extraordinary. Only four horsemen have jumped that gate in the last hundred years.'

'Really?'

'Their initials are carved in the gatepost.'

'Gosh. I thought it was high. That's quite a feat, then.'

'It is,' Kate agreed. 'Quite a feat. Jack's never tried it before and that's what surprises me.'

As Lizzie replaced the receiver she knew she should go straight to her room to start work. There were emails waiting for her, and hard work and efficiency had become a habit, a good habit she enjoyed.

And yet...this morning she felt a mysterious urge to abandon her desk and to wander outdoors... She wanted to breathe in the gentle autumn sunshine, to smell the roses, so to speak, although there probably weren't any roses in the neglected Savannah gardens.

She thought how soothing it would be to drink in the peaceful landscape, to admire the beautiful horses, and the never-ending plains and the wide open sky.

With the idea only half formed, Lizzie found herself on the veranda, and Cobber, Jack's elderly cattle dog, came bounding up the steps to greet her. He looked up at her with gentle, honey-brown eyes and she patted the soft fur on the top of his head.

She thought how comforting it must be to have a faithful dog as a constant companion. She'd never had a dog, but there'd always been cats and kittens in Monta Correnti and she'd spent many happy childhood hours with a warm, purring cat curled in her lap while she read, or day-dreamed.

Cobber followed her quietly as she went down the front steps and onto the grass. She caught an animal whiff from the horse paddock, but it was quite pleasant when it came mixed with the sweeter scent of hay.

A kookaburra on a fence post began to laugh and the comical, bubbling call brought a ready smile to her lips. She remembered the first time she'd ever heard a kookaburra, when she'd come to Australia at the age of eighteen. She'd been delighted. Still, all these years later, the sound never failed to make her smile.

She saw the silver threads of a spider's web hanging loosely between the branches of a neglected rose bush, and found one small, pretty pink rosebud. She was contemplating plucking it when Jack appeared around the corner of the shed.

His face broke into a smile, and a sweet pang speared her chest, spreading through her veins like a witch's potion. He looked more appealing than ever in his soft blue jeans and his faded shirt, and with a heavy, cumbersome saddle slung over his shoulder. As usual, he handled the saddle easily, as if it were as light as thistledown.

She thought—*He's like catnip for me. I can't stay away.*

But she spoke calmly as she said, 'Hello.' And her eyes wide with surprise as she tried to pretend he was the last person on the planet she expected to see.

'Good morning, Lizzie.'

'You look happy.'

'Actually, I'm feeling pretty damn good.'

'I—um—saw you take that gate. I was worried. I was sure you'd never make it. It looked too high.'

Jack nodded, smiling. 'Matter of fact, that gate is a challenge I've been avoiding for a long, long time.'

'But you took it this morning.'

'I did,' he said with a beaming smile. 'Piece of cake.'

Lizzie was so used to the chest-beating of politicians that she waited for Jack to brag about being one of only five riders who'd cleared the gate. But Jack wasn't like other men she'd known. No bragging for him.

No crowds to applaud his magnificent jump. No spraying champagne, or kisses from pretty girls.

He simply looked pleased and quietly happy, and, looking into his eyes, Lizzie couldn't help feeling pleased and happy, too.

In fact, happiness was fizzing through her like soda bubbles, and on a reckless impulse she took two steps towards him, grabbed a handful of his shirt, and kissed him on the mouth.

CHAPTER SIX

LIZZIE smiled into Jack's surprised eyes. 'There's no champagne, but you looked so pleased with yourself for clearing that jump, and I thought you ought to be congratulated.'

'Well, thank you, Senator.'

Before she could slip away, he reached around her, gripping her low on her behind, trapping her against his denim thighs, and next moment, he was answering her kiss with a kiss of his own.

And *his* kiss wasn't a mere smack on the lips.

His kiss was mesmerising, slow and thorough—a happy kiss, perfectly in tune with Lizzie's mood and with the beauty and brightness of the morning. He tasted of the clean, crisp outdoors, wild and untamed. He hadn't shaved, and his beard grazed her jaw, but she loved the maleness of it, just as she loved the faint hint of dust and saddle leather that clung to his clothing.

The saddle slid to the ground, landing with a thump and a clink of buckles. Jack pulled her closer and deepened the kiss, and she felt her desire blossom like a flower opening to the sun, while her good sense unravelled.

'Let's go inside,' he murmured, grazing kisses down the line of her jaw until her reasoning processes ceased to function.

In a warm and fuzzy daze, Lizzie allowed him to lead her, with a strong arm around her shoulders, to the steps. She knew he was planning to take her to his room, and she was struggling to remember why it wasn't wise. Why *should* she resist Jack?

How could she?

It wasn't till they turned down the hallway leading to Jack's room that she was finally stabbed by her reluctant guilty conscience. Of course, there were solid reasons why she shouldn't let this happen, and the main reason was becoming more evident every day.

Jack's kisses might feel wonderfully, perfectly right, and perhaps her feelings for him were more than a mere, mid-trimester spike in her hormones. But was her all-consuming need sufficient excuse to sleep with him?

In the doorway to his room, Lizzie's conscience began to shout. She stopped him with a hand on his arm. She had to be strong, had to be honest with him. It would be unconscionable to make love when Jack didn't know she was pregnant.

Bravely, she said, 'Jack, I'm sorry. This isn't a good idea.'

'Nonsense. It's the best idea you've had since you got here.'

She almost protested that it hadn't been her idea, but she knew that wasn't exactly honest. After all, she hadn't gone outside looking for fresh air and scenery. She'd been looking for Jack, hadn't she? And she'd more or less thrown herself into his arms.

'I'm sorry,' she said again, and with stronger emphasis. 'There's a reason we shouldn't do this, and I really should have told you.'

His forehead furrowed in a deep frown. 'What are you saying? What reason?'

Unable to meet the ferocity of his gaze, Lizzie looked through the doorway into his room. Which wasn't much help. She saw his king-size bed piled with pillows and a thick, comfy, black and grey striped duvet, and she fought off pictures of Jack lying there. With her. Kissing her all over.

She swallowed. 'Can we talk?'

He touched a thumb to the corner of her mouth. 'Sure. As soon as we've finished here.'

Lizzie wished her legs felt stronger. 'No, Jack. Can we go to the lounge room?'

'Not another talk in the lounge room.'

'Please.'

Jack gave a disbelieving shake of his head, but finally, tight-lipped, and without another word, he turned back down the hallway.

Shooting her a puzzled glance, he said, 'I suppose you're about to tell me exactly why you've come here.'

'Yes.' Lizzie had intended to sit down, to have a civilised conversation, just as they'd had last night, but she felt too agitated to sit still. 'I probably should have told you straight away.'

'I said I didn't need to know. It's none of my business why you're hiding.' Jack's throat rippled as he swallowed. 'Of course, that was before—' He stopped, clearly hesitating. His green eyes shimmered. 'Before I became attached to the idea of taking you to bed.'

Help. His words stirred all kinds of tremors inside her.

He said quietly, 'Is that what you're going to tell me? That there's a very good reason why I shouldn't take you to bed?'

Lizzie nodded. Her baby was the most important reason in the world for holding Jack at bay. Her longing for Jack might have temporarily got in the way, but her longing for her baby was much more important and meaningful than any physical yearning.

Her baby was everything. Her future. The sole focus of her love. The very best thing in her life.

Jack stood at the end of the sofa, hands thrust deep in his pockets, and she could feel his tension reaching across the room to her.

'There's something important I should have told you before this,' she said quietly.

'Speak up, Lizzie. I can't hear you.'

She turned, forcing herself to face him, knowing that what she had to say would for ever wipe the sexy sparkle from his eyes, but she didn't want him to think she was ashamed of the dear, precious baby growing inside her.

Lifting her chin, she said proudly and clearly, 'I'm pregnant.'

Pregnant?

Jack couldn't have been more surprised if Lizzie had announced she was a vampire. He felt as if the earth had slipped from beneath him.

'But—' He tried to speak, realised that he needed air, took a breath and tried again. 'But you told me last night there's no man in your life.'

'Well, yes, that's right.'

The anxious tremor in Lizzie's voice and her nervous pacing were *not* helping Jack's concentration.

'What's happened then? Has he left you?'

'No, Jack.'

Bewildered, he lifted a hand to scratch at his head. This was *not* making sense.

Lizzie stopped pacing and stood by the window, chewing her lip as she parted the curtain and looked out across

the sun-drenched landscape. Despite his shocked baffle-
ment, he could still taste her kiss, could smell the subtle
fragrance of her hair, could remember the happy burst of
longing he'd felt when she'd grabbed him and kissed him.
As if the floodgates had opened.

He longed to haul her back into his arms and kiss the
soft, sulky tilt of her mouth. Coax a smile.

She's not available.

She's pregnant.

The thought dug into him. *Pregnant.* His brain clamoured
with questions. *Who had made her pregnant? Why? When?*

Just looking at her, he couldn't tell that she was expecting, but he wondered now if the lush fullness of her breasts
and hips had been enhanced by the presence of her
growing baby.

A baby. For crying out loud, her body was a haven for
another man's child. How could she have told him there
was no man in her life?

Jack challenged her. 'There has to be a father.'

Lizzie turned from the window and gave a faint shake
of her head.

'Where is he?' Jack demanded.

'I don't know.'

'For God's sake, Lizzie, *who* is he, then?'

Her chin lifted a notch higher. 'I don't know his name.
All I can tell you is he's six feet three, and thirty-six years
old, and he's an engineer with an interest in classical music
and long-distance running.'

Jack's jaw sagged.

What the hell? How could she rattle off the guy's vital
statistics, yet claim that she didn't know his name?

'He's donor number 372,' she said tightly.

Donor?

Jack blinked. 'Your baby's father is a sperm donor?'

'Yes.'

Shock ripped through Jack. He was well acquainted with artificial insemination—it was a common practice in the cattle industry—but why would a hot-blooded, attractive woman like Lizzie need a clinical insemination? It didn't make sense.

He stared at her as she stood there, her flowing curves outlined against the rectangle of blue sky. He remembered her eagerness both this morning and last night.

Why would a beautiful, passionate woman like Lizzie Green reject a living, breathing lover and choose an anonymous donation in a syringe?

'Hell, Lizzie, if you wanted a baby, all you had to do was put the word out. Blokes would have been lining up.'

I would have been there at the head of the queue.

Jack grimaced, aware that after two kisses the possessiveness he felt for her was totally unjustified.

On the far side of the room, she leaned against the wall, looking down at her hands, twisting them anxiously. 'I hope I didn't sound flippant about the donor. The decision wasn't made lightly.'

'But it doesn't make sense.' Jack's voice rang loudly in the quiet room, echoing his confusion. 'How can an anonymous donor be the best option?'

A wistful smile tilted her mouth. 'That's not easy to explain. It's why I'm here at Savannah. Avoiding that very question, because I know that whatever I say, there'll be people who won't understand. I don't want journalists hounding me, asking stupid questions, blowing my story out of proportion and whipping up the public's emotions.'

'But you can't hide here for ever. You'll have to explain eventually.'

'Yes.' Arms crossed, Lizzie drew a deep breath, let it out slowly. 'I just wanted time to get used to being pregnant, and to make sure everything's OK with the baby before I face the music. Ideally, I'd keep this quiet until the baby's safely delivered.'

'Is there much chance of that?'

Lizzie shrugged. 'Unfortunately, I can't hide for ever. But I'm sure people will react differently when there's a real live baby to show them, but right now the focus will be on the whys and hows of the pregnancy, and most people can't understand why I chose to go solo.'

And who could blame most people? Jack thought grimly. 'I can't promise to understand, but I'd like to hear your explanation,' he said.

Her smile was doubtful. 'Of course.'

At least she came back to sit on the couch.

Jack sat, too. At the opposite end.

In a perfect world, Lizzie would have kicked off her shoes and tucked her legs beneath her, settling in for a cosy, heart-to-heart chat.

No, in a perfect world she would have been in his arms, continuing where their kiss left off.

Instead, she began to trace the leafy pattern of the upholstery with her forefinger. 'It's hard to know where to start. It's not as if I woke up one morning and thought I'd like to have a sperm-donor baby. The idea more or less evolved.'

She lifted a hand to rub her brow as if it would help to clarify her thoughts. 'I'd been so focused on my career, you see, and on other people's problems. Throw in a couple of unlucky love affairs, and I was nearing forty before I realised I was missing out on things that were really important to *me*.'

'Like a family?'

'Yes, a family.'

'But most women start with a partner.'

Lizzie nodded. 'That was my dream once, to find a partner first, then have a baby.'

'But?' Jack gestured for her to answer.

Lizzie hesitated.

'Don't tell me you've never found another man to step into MacCallum's shoes.'

'Oh, I found one, all right. Problem was, he fitted those shoes only too well.' Her eyes glinted with the threat of tears, but she managed a shaky smile. 'An upwardly mobile corporate banker. Head of a couple of investment companies. We were together twelve months and I thought he was serious.'

Her mouth opened as if she was about to say more, then changed her mind. 'Can I ask you a question, Jack?'

'Sure.'

'Why aren't you married?'

'I— I—' An uncomfortable sensation blocked his throat. He swallowed. 'I guess I haven't looked all that hard, but—' he shrugged '—I haven't found the right woman.'

'Exactly. And I haven't found anyone I was happy to marry, but I chose a donor because I'm fussy. Not because there were no men available.'

Her mouth twisted in an embarrassed smile. 'It's really hard to talk about this to a man, especially after—'

'After we've just kissed each other into tomorrow,' Jack supplied in a grating tone. 'What was that about, Lizzie? Don't tell me you were simply happy to see me.'

The colour in her cheeks deepened. 'You jumped the gate—and I got caught up in the moment—and then we got a bit carried away.'

Blushing, she stared at a spot on the carpet. 'I said I'm sorry, Jack.'

He shrugged. There was no point in carrying on like a

whipped puppy. He had no doubt that Lizzie enjoyed a wide circle of friends and acquaintances, and it was sobering to know that she hadn't found one guy who measured up to her high standards. Damn it, how high were these standards anyway?

He was still mulling over this when she said, 'The thing is I simply wasn't prepared to marry some poor unsuspecting man just because I wanted a baby.' She met his gaze and her hazel eyes flashed. 'It's not a very honest reason to tie the knot, is it?'

What could Jack say? 'I—I guess not.'

'I gave it a lot of thought,' she added, finally kicking off her shoes, as if she could relax now that her confession was complete.

Unhappily, Jack watched as she curled into her corner of the sofa with the unconscious grace of a cat. He thought about the way he'd thundered back to the homestead this morning, confident that he should try again with her.

Arriving at that decision had felt good, *really* good, and he'd taken the stockyard gate in a burst of triumph, and then Lizzie had met him, her face glowing, full of smiles and kisses...

Now, she began to speak again, earnestly, as if she felt compelled to explain and justify every reason why their kiss had been a mistake.

'Single mothers can do a great job. My mother's a prime example. She gave my sisters and me a very happy childhood. Being raised by a good single mum has to be better than being raised in a bad marriage.'

Jack couldn't argue with that. His parents' marriage had been desperately unhappy, and his childhood had been blighted by their endless fights and arguments. He could remember lying in bed at night, head beneath the pillow, fingers jammed in his ears, trying to shut out their bitter, angry voices.

'What about your father?' he said. 'Was he happy for your mother to keep you to herself?'

'Actually, no.' Lizzie dropped her gaze. 'Not that I knew much about my father when I was a child. It was only later when I came to live with him that I realised how hurt and excluded he'd felt. That's another reason I settled on a sperm donor. Knowing how Dad felt, I knew that an affair with someone just to create a baby would cause all sorts of emotional fallout.'

No question about that, Jack thought. Lots of guys took being a father pretty seriously.

After the rough time he'd had with his old man, he'd spent a lot of time thinking about the fatherhood role. He couldn't deny that some fathers were jerks, but all his married mates were nuts about their kids, and he'd always reckoned that he would be, too, when his turn came.

'So,' Lizzie said, watching him carefully. 'That's my story. I—I hope you understand.'

Jack swallowed. He hated the thought of Lizzie facing parenthood alone. It seemed such a waste. But, clearly, it was none of his business.

'You put up a fair case,' he said.

'That's good to know.'

'But this doesn't mean you're staying clear of men for ever, does it?'

Her eyes widened with surprise. 'I—ah—haven't made any plans past my baby's delivery.'

A pulse thundered in Jack's throat. Lizzie mightn't have made plans, but he'd had plans. His plans had involved exploring every inch of her luscious skin. He'd planned to make love to her with finesse and passion.

Now his plans were toast, and this morning's notions were nothing but a bag of bulldust. Hell, there was no point in even thinking about getting closer. Lizzie was focused on her baby. She didn't need or want a man in her life. And why would he want to be there, anyway?

Why would he want to be involved with a woman who came with so much baggage—a headache career, and now a baby that wouldn't even know its own dad?

No, thank you.

Jack cleared his throat, eager to put an end to this conversation. 'If I sounded critical, I apologise. I spoke out of turn. You have every right to make your own decisions. It's your life, your baby.'

He stood quickly, forced a quick smile as he tried to ignore the tempting picture she made, curled on the sofa, tanned legs glowing, dark hair shining in a stream of sunlight. 'I'm sure you're busy.' Already, he was heading for the door. 'So I'll let you get on with your work.'

It was time to get out of here.

His previously hazy reasons for staying clear of Lizzie were multiplying madly and already he was telling himself he'd had a lucky escape. It was time to get out of there before he said or did something foolish. There was no point in turning a bad situation into a flaming disaster.

CHAPTER SEVEN

STANDING at the open doorway of her room, Lizzie looked at the sunburnt plains, while she applied herself to the extraordinarily difficult task of *not* missing Jack.

He'd headed off somewhere to work, and she'd come here to her room—to *work*—but it was proving impossible. Jack was front, back and centre of her thoughts.

No doubt he was puzzled and possibly upset after she'd rushed out to greet him with kisses, then retreated, and promptly delivered the news of her pregnancy.

How could she have been so irresponsible? She prided herself on her prudence. She'd never been reckless around men. Well…not after she'd learned two very difficult lessons. But now, to her shame, she couldn't stop thinking about Jack's kiss.

Even though she'd stopped it, and delivered a speech that ensured it would never be repeated, he'd ignited a craving in her.

Lizzie knew it was wrong. Regret was such a useless emotion.

She'd never been a thrill-seeker, had never been bothered by any kind of addiction, not even to chocolate, but now every cell in her body screamed for the return of

Jack's lips. She wanted his mouth, teasing and warm, on her skin. She longed for—

Enough.

Angry at her weakness, she whirled away from the doorway, sat down at her desk and clicked on her Internet connection. Listening to the internal whirring of her laptop, she watched a raft of emails download. Her heart leapt when she saw a different name sitting in the middle of the familiar addresses of work colleagues.

Isabella Casali. Her cousin. At last, a message from Monta Correnti.

Lizzie smiled with relief as she opened the message. She'd been worried.

The message was in English. Isabella was proud of her language skills and loved to use English whenever she could.

Dearest Lizzie,

I'm sorry I haven't answered your emails before now. Papa's not at all well, so I'm in charge of 'Rosa', and we've been really busy. I've been run off my feet.

I hope you and your baby are fine, and keeping well. Are you still holed up in that place in the outback? It must be fascinating. A totally different world.

Now, let me tell you about Max. Forgive me, Lizzie, while I have a small rave. Max is wonderful. I'm so happy. I can't believe how sweet he is to me. His love still feels like a miracle.

A miracle. Lizzie sensed a wealth of happiness in Isabella's word choice and she was really pleased for her cousin, but she also felt an inexplicable stab of jealousy.

I'm afraid I haven't seen your mother. I've been too busy.

And too upset with my mother, Lizzie thought. Fair enough, too.

So far, there has been no news of the twins. As you know, I really wanted to go to New York to find them, but Papa can't spare me. Actually, this message will have to be brief as I have so much to do, and there's a problem in the kitchen.
I'll try harder to keep in touch.
Ciao,
Isabella.

Lizzie let out a sigh of relief, pleased to finally have contact from someone at home. After all these years in Australia, she still thought of Monta Correnti as her home.

If only her family could be more harmonious.

She thought of her mother—stunningly beautiful, fiercely independent, still harbouring deep resentment towards her half-brother, Luca.

It was such a pity. Why was she still so angry, after all this time? Why couldn't she let go?

On an impulse, Lizzie dialled her mother's number, but she only got her answering machine. She left a brief message. 'Thinking of you, Mama. Love you. I'm well. Please get in touch when you're free. *Ciao*.'

Over the next few days, Lizzie saw very little of Jack. He seemed to be extra busy with station work and she kept busy, too, working at her desk, and taking short morning walks and even shorter afternoon rests. She told herself that she was pleased at last to be able to give her full attention to the books she'd brought.

Jack's busyness was a good thing. This distancing from

each other was highly desirable. It was exactly what she needed. Now she could focus on her work and her baby, the two things that mattered.

Everything else, including Jack, was a distraction. She only wished she didn't have to tell herself this so many times. Every day.

She saw Jack at mealtimes, of course, and they continued to share the cooking. But while they talked easily about their different worlds, and she felt they both enjoyed getting to know more and more about each other, Jack was careful to keep any inference of flirtation out of their conversation. There were no stolen kisses. No sparkling glances. No touching.

It was a shock to learn that, despite the endless lectures she'd given herself, she missed the sizzle that had simmered between them. It was hard, *really* hard to let it go. To her dismay, she still found Jack incredibly attractive.

Too often, way too often, she had wicked fantasies.

One afternoon, she was busy answering an email from Canberra when she heard Jack's footsteps on the veranda, and she froze, fingers poised above the keyboard, listening with her full attention.

He went past her room, and turned into his room, and she heard his shower taps turn on. She tried—honestly, she *did* try—to stop herself from imagining him standing there, naked. She tried not to picture the soap bubbles sliding over his shiny bronzed shoulders, slipping down his muscly chest. Then lower.

Heat flared like tiny bushfires inside her. The picture of Jack sprang into painfully clear focus. She could see the gleaming slickness of his wet skin stretched over bands of muscles. She thought how blissfully liberating it would be to run her hands over his bare back, then over his front.

It wasn't till the sound of the water stopped abruptly that her common sense slammed a door on her thoughts.

For heaven's sake, how could she have forgotten so much, so quickly? Why was it so hard to remember she was a forty-year-old, pregnant woman, who'd chosen, yes, *chosen* to be a single mother?

Three evenings later, after another carefully polite and unsatisfactory dinner conversation, she ran into Jack. Literally.

It happened in the hallway, when she was coming back from the bathroom, after a long and supposedly calming soak in the tub. She'd wrapped a towel around her wet hair and she was wearing her white towelling bathrobe—nothing else—and her skin was warm and flushed and smelling of rose and lavender bath oil.

She'd used up almost all of Kate's collection of bath oils, and she'd made a note to try to buy some more.

She'd been reading in the bath till her toes were frilly, and she was carrying the thick paperback novel back to her room, intending to continue reading in bed. She had her head down, checking that she'd marked her place, when she banged into Jack.

The book fell to the floor.

'Sorry!' they both cried at once, and simultaneously they both stooped to retrieve the book.

What happened then was quite strange, like something out of a movie. Lizzie was bending down, conscious that her bath robe was gaping, revealing quite a bit of her cleavage, pink and perfumed from her bath, but instead of feeling embarrassed, or coy, instead of modestly adjusting the robe, she was frozen, as still as a statue, mesmerised by Jack.

He was kneeling inches from her, and they were both holding her book, staring at each other, breathing unevenly as if they'd run a hard race.

She could feel his heat, enveloping her like a mysterious fog, and they rose in slow motion, still holding the book. In unison, Jack took a step towards her and she took a step back, and it was like dancing a slow waltz.

Lizzie found herself against the cool paintwork of the hallway, holding her book. Trapped by Jack. His hands were now on the wall, on either side of her head, and she had stopped breathing.

Stopped thinking, had become nothing but a mass of wanting.

He was close. So close. Touching close. Kissing close. She could see each individual pinprick of his beard, and the surprising softness of his lips.

Her body was hot and tight with wanting.

Through the open neck of her bathrobe, Jack's fingers traced her skin, burning a trail from her throat to between her breasts, making her gasp.

'Lizzie,' he whispered and he smiled directly into her eyes. 'You know you only have to ask.' His mouth brushed a nerve-tingling, fiery sweep over her lips.

Then he stepped away, turned down the hallway, and disappeared into the darkness.

Somehow, Lizzie made her way back to her room, where she fell in a trembling mess onto her bed. She was shocked by the strength of her desire for Jack, by the force of her aching, physical longing.

You only have to ask…

She wasn't going to ask. She couldn't possibly ask, could she? She was so much older than he was, and pregnant. How could he find her desirable?

You only have to ask…

His words wouldn't leave her alone. They danced in her

head like haunting, beautiful music. Like tendrils of en-chanted smoke, they curled around her heart.

Only have to ask...

The idea was so alluring. Jack was so disturbingly at-tractive, and she'd been alone for so long.

But it was a mistake for all kinds of reasons. It was, wasn't it?

Wasn't it?

With one touch, Jack had destroyed her certainty.

Jack couldn't quite believe he'd said that to Lizzie.

You only have to ask.

Fool. He needed his head read.

Except...he hadn't been thinking with his head.

Lizzie had been there, practically naked, fresh from the bath and smelling of every temptation known to man, her skin so soft and pink and warm, her mouth trembling in anticipation of his kiss.

Thank God he'd managed to resist.

There was now a long list of ways she was wrong for him. After a childhood locked in a rigid career pattern, he was finally happy with his life. Why spoil it by getting involved with Lizzie and the complications of her high profile career, her ambition, her lifestyle, her pregnancy with another man's baby?

Problem was, he knew all that, but he still wanted her like crazy.

You only have to ask.

As if she would ask. He might be a fool, but Lizzie had her head screwed on.

And yet...

He'd seen the flash of disappointment in her eyes

when he'd backed away. If he were a gambling man, he'd bet that he still had a chance.

That evening there was an email from Isabella. Lizzie clicked on it eagerly, keen for more news of her family and relieved to be distracted from her latest dilemmas over Jack.

Hi Lizzie,
I have such good news and I'm so excited. I've managed to track down Alessandro and Angelo's contact details, and I'm going to send emails introducing myself as their sister.
Actually, there's some other news, but I'm not sure that I should tell you.

Lizzie's heart gave a sickening thud when she read this sentence. She closed her eyes, not wanting to read the rest of Isabella's message. In her everyday life, she never avoided bad news, but this was different, this was family, and she felt a flicker of fear like the darting of a snake's tongue.
She opened her eyes and kept reading.

My father told me something today, something very disturbing. I'm sorry, Lizzie. I'm afraid it concerns Lisa.
I guess you're bound to hear some time, so I wanted to warn you, but I think it would be better if you heard it from your mother.
I hope I'm not scaring you, Lizzie. It's not an emergency. Your mother isn't sick. But I think you should ask her to explain her behaviour when my father went to her for help. I'm sorry if that sounds terribly cryptic, but that's all I want to say at the moment.
Love,
Isabella.

Appalled, Lizzie read the message again, trying to make sense of it. Ask her to explain her behaviour when my father went to her for help.

What could her mother have done?

Acid rose, filling Lizzie's throat.

As a child, she'd idolised her mother. Lisa Firenzi was regally beautiful, strongly independent, and the successful owner of Monta Correnti's most sophisticated restaurant. Lizzie's ideal woman.

Even after Lizzie had come to Australia to be close to her father, she'd modelled herself on Lisa. Her mother's example of self-sufficiency and feminine triumph was the one thing that had saved Lizzie when Mitch MacCallum had so heartlessly thrown her aside. It had helped again years later when Toby the banker had caused so much grief.

There'd been many times during her political career when Lizzie had used Lisa's strength as inspiration.

Without her mother as a role model, she might never have embarked on this pregnancy…

But what have you done, Mama?

It was a question she hardly dared to ask, but, unhappily, she knew she had no choice. Lizzie knew she must ask it, even though she was positive she wouldn't like the answer.

Her hands were shaking as she picked up her phone and began to press the buttons.

CHAPTER EIGHT

JACK stopped outside Lizzie's bedroom door.

He thought he'd heard crying, but that was impossible. Lizzie was so strong. He'd seen that with his own eyes, and he'd been reading on the Internet about her reputation for being a particularly tough senator.

Apparently, Lizzie had rarely let the opposition break her down, and he couldn't imagine her collapsing into a fit of weeping, but when he leaned closer to the door there could be no mistake. Lizzie was definitely crying. No, it was worse than that. She was sobbing uncontrollably, as if her heart would break.

Alarmed, Jack tapped on her door, but she was crying so loudly she couldn't hear him. He gave the door a gentle push, and it swung forward to reveal Lizzie sprawled on her bed, abandoned in misery, her face red, tear-stained, twisted with despair, her body shaking.

The sight sliced into Jack. At first he was too shocked to think, but then he raced through possibilities.

Was there a problem with the baby? A miscarriage?

He felt a slug of fear, but almost immediately reasoned that if there were pregnancy complications Lizzie would have come to him for help. She was too smart to suffer in silence. She would have asked him to take her to a doctor.

No, this had to be something else. Worse? Jack couldn't bear to see her like this. His impulse was to sweep her into his arms, to hold her close, to soothe her, as if she were a child. But he was uncomfortably aware that she wouldn't welcome such intimacy from him.

Uncertain and anxious, he hovered near the end of her bed. His eyes hunted her room for clues. It was all very tidy. Nothing appeared to be amiss. Her laptop had been turned off, but there was a mobile phone lying on the bed beside her. He wondered if she'd heard bad news.

Abruptly, as if she'd sensed his presence, she lifted her head and saw him, and then she sat up quickly, her hands flying to swipe at her tears.

'I'm sorry to disturb you,' Jack said. 'But I couldn't help hearing how upset you were and I was worried. I was hoping I might be able to help somehow.'

She swiped again at her tear-streaked face. 'That's kind, but no. It's just—' Her face crumpled and she gestured frantically towards her desk in the corner. 'Could you pass me that box of tissues?'

Jack did so quickly, and she pulled out a great wad of tissues and mopped at her face and blew her nose. When she'd finished, she dumped the damp clump on the bedside table, and tried, unsuccessfully, to smile.

'I must look a fright.'

'I don't scare easily.' He was relieved. Things couldn't be too disastrous if Lizzie was worried about her appearance. 'Anyway, a red nose looks good on you.'

This time she did manage a faint, shaky smile.

'Are you sure there's nothing I can do, Lizzie?'

She shook her head. 'It's just—' Her hands flapped in a gesture of helplessness. 'My crazy family in Italy. Sometimes I just want to—'

She stopped, and sat there looking lost, and Jack's heart went out to her. Everything about her sent a message of huge need—the deep emotion in her eyes, the vulnerable droop of her shoulders, the lingering tremor of her soft lips, her hands now twisting a tissue to shreds.

When she looked up directly into his eyes, he read a silent entreaty to take her in his arms, to kiss away her tears, to sweep her away from whatever was troubling her.

Or was he getting carried away?

Prudently, he remained still. It would be all too easy to take advantage of Lizzie's vulnerability—but right now he simply wanted to help her.

He cleared his throat. 'Can I get you something? A cup of tea?'

Inside, he winced. He sounded like a doddering aunt who believed all the world's problems could be solved by a cup of tea.

Lizzie looked surprised, too. She blinked at him. 'Tea would be lovely. Thank you, Jack.'

'Hang in there,' he said gently. 'I'll be back in two shakes.'

She gave him a bleak smile. 'I'll go wash my face.'

Lizzie hurried to the bathroom, filled the basin with warm water, and washed her face with liberal splashes.

Normally, she hated to cry, but tonight after her phone call to her mother, she'd felt so alone, she'd more or less collapsed. Now, with her face washed and patted dry, she was already better. Cleansed. Calmer.

She took a cautious glimpse in the mirror, saw that her eyes and nose were still red and swollen.

At least she felt more composed. Actually, she'd begun to calm down when she'd discovered Jack standing at the end of her bed. He'd looked wonderful standing there, so tall and handsome and reliable in his old blue jeans and a faded brown countryman's shirt. A steadying anchor.

She was very grateful that he'd braved her closed door and come in. His strong, companionable presence had made her feel suddenly safe and she'd wanted to fall into his arms, to dry her tears on his shirtfront, to bury her face against his shoulder.

It would have been perfect. With Jack's arms about her, she would have felt comforted, safe again, rescued from that awful feeling that she'd lost her bearings.

But Jack had kept his distance. He'd been friendly and kind and concerned—and distant—and shame on her for expecting anything else. This was what she'd demanded of him—to be a friend, not her lover. She knew she should be grateful. She *was* enormously grateful.

Now she stared hard at her reflection. *Come on, Lizzie. Shoulders back. You're strong, remember.*

She still didn't feel particularly strong as she went back to her room, where Jack very soon joined her with two mugs of tea.

'You should make yourself comfy,' he told her, in a kindly tone.

So she sat on Kate Burton's comfortable bed, with the pillows plumped up, and her legs, in slim cream Capri pants, stretched out in front of her. Jack swung the chair out from her desk and sat there, on the far side of the room, with an ankle propped on a knee.

'That chair looks too small for you, Jack.'

He sent a cursory glance to her bed, the only other place in the room, apart from the floor, where he could sit. 'This chair's fine, thanks.'

Lizzie dropped her gaze, and took a sip of her tea. It was very hot and strong and sweet, exactly what she needed.

'You're looking better,' he said. 'Not so pale.'

'I'm feeling much better, thank you.' She drank more tea, then smiled at him. 'You're a really nice man. You know that, don't you?'

'I hear it from the stockmen every day.'

They shared a grin and as they sat there, drinking tea in the quiet house, Lizzie found herself wanting to tell him about her family and why she'd been so upset.

'Do you mind if I talk? Get it off my chest?'

'Of course not.'

'I suppose it's a female thing—needing to offload emotional baggage.'

'As long as you don't think of me as a girlfriend.'

'Fat chance.'

Settling against the pillows, she began to tell him about her family, about the two rivalling family restaurants, Rosa and Sorella, and the tensions that seemed to have existed for ever, and about her uncle Luca and the twins, and how Isabella had always worked so very hard.

'But tonight, it got so much worse,' she said. 'There was an email from Isabella, telling me to ring my mother. So I did.'

Tears threatened, and Lizzie took a deep breath. 'It seems Luca's first wife, Cindy, went back to America, leaving him with their twins. He was struggling financially, so he asked my mother for help, for money.'

She closed her eyes, remembering the coldness in her mother's voice as soon as Luca's name was mentioned. All the usual warmth had vanished. It was like turning off a switch.

'My mother refused to help him.' Lizzie's voice broke on a sob, and she reached for the tissues and blew her nose.

'Maybe she had good reasons for refusing,' Jack suggested gently.

Lizzie shook her head. 'Luca's her brother, Jack. What kind of sister would refuse to help her own brother? I know the two of them have always fought like cats and dogs, but this was inexcusable. She's always had plenty of money, and Luca was struggling. How could she turn him away empty-handed? He had two little mouths to feed. But my mother, their aunt, wouldn't help and—'

Tears chased each other down Lizzie's cheeks. 'He had to send Alessandro and Angelo away to America because he couldn't afford to feed them.' Her voice rose on a note of horror. 'And it was my mother's fault.'

She could still picture those bright, eager little boys with their shiny eyes and cheeky smiles. It would have broken Luca's heart to give them up, to willingly separate himself from his sons. And now they'd been gone for so long.

Her mother's lack of compassion shocked Lizzie to the core. She felt betrayed by the person she loved most.

Twice in her life she'd loved and admired someone so much that she'd allowed that person to shape her life. Those two people had been Mitch MacCallum and Lisa Firenzi.

First Mitch had let her down badly, and tonight Lizzie felt as if her mother had pulled her very foundations from beneath her feet.

Such a big part of her decision to have a sperm-donor pregnancy stemmed from her certainty that her mother would approve and applaud her. Now she wondered why Lisa's opinion had seemed so damned important.

Nothing made sense any more.

Setting aside her mug, Lizzie sent Jack a shaky smile. She felt drained by her confession. 'You probably think I'm making a mountain out of a molehill.'

'Not at all,' he said. 'It's never easy to accept flaws in someone you love.'

Jack understood. He really understood. She'd momentarily forgotten his problems with his father, but, of course, he probably understood a great deal. Knowing that, and sitting here with him now, in her bedroom, wrapped by the silent outback night, she felt astonishingly close to him.

They talked on, sharing stories about their childhood, about their parents, and the difficulties of accepting that idols too often had feet of clay. They even talked, eventually, about the possibility of forgiveness, and Lizzie found the idea extremely comforting.

She would have liked to go on talking for ages, but when she yawned Jack stood and collected their mugs.

'Thanks so much for the tea and the talk,' she said, hoping she didn't sound too disappointed.

He looked down at her, an ambiguous expression in his gorgeous green eyes. 'You'd better get some sleep.'

He was leaving and she felt suddenly, desperately lonely. Truly lonely. It made no sense. To be alone was what she wanted—to be single and solitary and strong.

Like her mother.

Oh, help.

Jack's voice whispered in her head. *You only have to ask.*

On impulse, she reached for his free hand. 'Do you have to go?'

He went very still. 'Are you asking me to stay?'

'Yes, I think I am.' She held her breath. She couldn't believe she was doing this. Jack had said that she only had to ask, but how could she be sure he really wanted her? He was so hunky and fit and ten years younger. She was pregnant.

Embarrassment flamed her cheeks as she remembered the recent changes in her body. She'd always been full-breasted, but now her breasts were bigger than ever, and heavy. Her baby bulge was becoming noticeable, too.

Silently, Jack set the mugs down on the small bedside table, then sat on the edge of her bed. Her heart thudded as the mattress dipped beneath his weight. She caught the faint drift of soap on his skin, saw that his green eyes were clouded with a smoky mix of wariness and desire.

His throat rippled as he swallowed, and the air in the room seemed to tremble.

Nervous flutters danced in Lizzie's stomach. After the way she'd turned Jack away in the past, she couldn't really blame him if he got to his feet again and walked out the door.

'If I stay, I'll want to make love to you, Lizzie.'

Her throat was so full she couldn't speak, could only nod.

The caution in his eyes gave way to his trademark sparkle. He hadn't shaved and her fingertips touched the masculine roughness of his beard.

She smiled. 'You're so lovely and whiskery.'

His hand captured hers, and he kissed her fingers. 'You're so lovely and silky.' Leaning in, he kissed her lips. 'And you're so soft.' He kissed her again, gently at first, and then with open-mouthed thoroughness. 'Lizzie... I love the way you taste.'

'How do I taste?'

'Like moonlight. Perfect.'

'You taste of sunlight. Perfect too.'

He smiled. 'Night and day.'

Their kiss deepened and he gathered her in to him, nipping, tasting, delving. Happiness flowed through her. For too long she'd lived in a vacuum of touch, but now Jack's hands were making dreamy circles on her arms, on her back, over her throat, her shoulders, and his mouth was awakening a thousand forgotten pleasures.

When he began to undo the buttons on her blouse she

was no longer nervous, but rosy and warm, edgy with ex-cited anticipation.

Her blouse fell open, and the night air was cool on her skin, and she closed her eyes as he kissed a sweet line from her throat down her chest.

But when he removed her bra her eyes snapped open, and she felt compelled to explain. 'My breasts have changed. Because of the baby. I hope you don't mind.'

Gently, almost reverently, he tested their weight in his hands. 'You're beautiful, Lizzie. Amazing. More perfec-tion.' He lowered his head, bestowing the softest of kisses. 'But I don't want to hurt you.'

'You won't.' Already, desire was sweeping her coyness aside. 'Don't worry. I'm fine and so is the baby.'

'More than fine.' Jack's voice was thick and choked, and when he kissed her again any lingering shreds of doubt were exploded by her gathering desire and excited certainty.

She needed this. Every touch, every kiss was vitally, cru-cially important, and so very right for her.

Jack was right for her, so good to her, and she needed his loving. So much. Too much.

Morning. Jack watched the gentle sunlight filter through the curtains as he lay beside Lizzie, and his heart seemed to spin with happiness. What a lovely sight she was, with her cheeks warm with sleep and her dark hair a messed-up tumble on the pillow.

He still found it hard to believe that last night had hap-pened. He'd known at the outset that Lizzie was primarily seeking comfort, but to his surprise she'd responded with stunning sweetness and passion, and it had seemed to him that she'd given so much more than she'd taken. This morn-ing he was floating.

Unable to resist, he dropped a kiss onto her soft, sexy lips. She opened her eyes and smiled.

'Hey there,' she said softly.

'Hey to you.'

She yawned and stretched and smiled again. 'Wow. I'm remembering last night. It was amazing, wasn't it?'

'It was,' he agreed, and he kissed her bare shoulder. 'So are you and your baby OK?' He had to ask. He felt incredibly protective now.

'We're fabulous, Jack.' Lizzie met his gaze shyly. 'Thank you.'

Smiling, she slid her hand down her body, her marvellous, lush body, and let it rest on the gentle swell of her abdomen and the secret miracle inside her. 'I dreamed about her last night.'

'About the baby?'

'Yes. I dreamed I could see right inside, and she was curled up like a sweet little fern frond. She had dark eyes and tiny, perfect arms and legs, and tiny fingers and toes, just like the pictures in the medical books.'

'Wow.'

'It was so reassuring.'

'A good dream, then.'

'The best.'

'Do you already know you're having a girl?'

The lips he'd kissed so thoroughly last night pouted. 'Actually, no I don't know the baby's sex yet, but in the dream she was definitely a girl and I was so pleased. I called her Madeline, and now I feel certain that I'm going to have a girl.'

'I can picture you with a daughter.'

'So can I.' Lizzie grinned. 'It feels right. I grew up with sisters and no brothers, so I think I'll feel much more comfortable with a little girl.'

To Jack's dismay he found that he was jealous of this little girl who was not and never would be his daughter. He pushed the thought aside. 'Madeline's a pretty name.'

'It's a very feminine name, isn't it?'

'I guess.' To cover his feeling of exclusion, he resorted to teasing. 'But I thought you'd consider names like Cleopatra, or Boadicea.'

'Why would I want to call my poor baby—?' Lizzie stopped and watched him closely, then laughed. 'Oh, right. Sure. I should follow my mother's example and name my daughter after a strong woman.'

'Italians like to follow family traditions, don't they?'

'Not this Italian.' She gave his arm a playful punch. 'Anyway, I'm half Australian.'

'So you are.' Possessively, Jack traced her silky smooth hip. 'I wonder which half of you is Italian and which half is Australian.'

When she began to laugh, he stopped her with a kiss. 'I'd be willing to bet that your lips are Italian.'

She groaned softly. 'Jack, no. Please don't start seducing me now.'

'Why not?'

'I can't spend all morning in bed.'

'Of course you can.'

'I can't. I have a mountain of work to get through today, and I can't undo the good habits of a lifetime in a single day.'

'Why not?' he asked again, and he began to kiss her. All over.

'Because—'

He touched her with his tongue and she let out a soft whimper.

'You're right,' she said in a breathless whisper. 'Why not?'

* * *

If she concentrated, Lizzie could get on with her work. Except…every so often she simply had to stop…to remember how happy she was…and how truly perfect Jack's loving had been.

She'd felt perfectly safe entrusting her body to him, and he'd taken her with just the right balance of tenderness and passion, so that she'd felt totally free and relaxed and uninhibited, and everything had been—in a word—

Blissful.

That evening the Savannah paddocks were bathed in a soft purple twilight that matched the gathering silence as, one by one, the bird calls stopped, and the sun slowly sank, bleeding streaks of crimson into the western sky.

In the kitchen, Lizzie was running late. Having worked too long after her late-morning start, she'd almost forgotten it was her turn to cook, and now she was busy throwing together a last-minute scratch meal. Curried chickpeas, a staple from her university days, was something she still served in rare emergencies. It involved little more than a diced onion and garlic thrown into a pan with a handful of spices, a can of chickpeas and another of tomatoes.

Normally, Lizzie served it with naan bread, but the Savannah pantry didn't run to packets of reheatable naan, so she steamed rice instead, and hoped Jack wouldn't mind a vegetarian meal.

She was listening to jazz on the radio, something she hadn't done for years. A blues tune, slow and moody with a saxophone crooning and a double bass deeply plucking the beat. The music soothed her, as did the aromatic fragrance of the spices, and she thought with a sense of wonder that she couldn't remember the last time she'd felt so calm and deeply happy.

'Something smells delicious.'

At the sound of Jack's voice she turned from the stove.

It was the first time she'd seen him since he'd left her bed and she felt a sweet pang, exactly as if an arrow had speared her heart. She also felt just a little bit coy, but Jack was, as always, completely at ease, and he flipped her a friendly grin.

'You say the food smells delicious every night I cook.'

'Because you always cook something delicious.'

'Or because you're always ravenous.'

'That too.' After a beat, he said, 'Cool music. That's Fox Bones, isn't it?'

'Who?'

'Fox Bones, on the sax.'

'Oh? I'm not sure.' She shot him a curious smile. 'Do you like jazz?'

'Sure. It's my favourite kind of music.'

'I had you pegged as a country and western fan.'

'I thought you'd be an opera buff. All those Italians. Pavarotti.'

Lizzie shrugged. 'He's good, but I prefer Fox Bones.'

They exchanged happy grins.

Jack came closer, shooting a curious glance at the contents of her frying pan. 'That's not Italian, is it?'

'I've pretty much exhausted my Italian repertoire.' She felt compelled to warn him. 'Tonight it's chickpeas.'

He nodded. 'Chickpeas and—?'

'And rice.'

'And what kind of meat?'

'No meat, Jack.'

He stared at her.

'It doesn't hurt to have an occasional meatless meal,' she said defensively.

'Says who?'

'The health experts.' Lizzie was about to expand on the theme of a balanced diet when she caught the cheeky gleam in Jack's eyes.

Was he teasing her again?

Apparently, yes. When she served the meal, he tucked into it with enthusiasm.

She thought, *I'm getting too used to this companionship sharing leisurely meals without being interrupted by a phone call or having to rush off to a meeting…having someone to talk to about everyday things that have nothing to do with work…looking forward to seeing him at the end of each day…*

As if he could read her thoughts, Jack said suddenly, 'I was wondering about your plans, Lizzie.'

'My plans?'

He smiled cautiously. 'You know—how long you'll be staying here, and what you're going to do when you leave.'

To her dismay she was suddenly flustered and stammering. 'I—I—well, you see—I have to be back in Canberra next month.'

'What happens then?'

'Senate will be in session. That's what I'm preparing for now. There's so much reading to get through, and all sorts of preliminary discussions by email.'

'But after the session?'

'After?'

'Yes,' he said with quiet insistence.

'I have a decision to make.'

Jack's eyes widened.

She knew she should explain. 'I won't be able to keep the

pregnancy a secret, so I'll have to decide whether I'll carry
on with my current responsibilities and face the barrage of
questions from the press, or resign and slip quietly away to
have my baby out of the limelight. In Italy perhaps.'

'If I were you, I'd be taking the second option.'

Lizzie fiddled with her water glass. 'That would certainly be the easy way out. But as a politician, I feel almost
duty-bound to stay in the senate, to be a sort of advocate,
I guess, for single women's rights.'

'They don't need you. It's too much to take on. Too much
pressure can't be good for you when you're pregnant.'

'That's true.' Before she could say anything more, the
phone rang in Jack's study, down the hall.

He let out a huff of irritation. 'I suppose I'd better go
and answer that.' Already, he was on his feet. 'Excuse me.'

After he'd gone, Lizzie stared at his almost-empty plate
thinking about the way his face had sobered as she'd talked
about the future. She couldn't expect him to understand
that her career had to come first.

She was proud of her fierce commitment to her elector-
ate, and she couldn't let one night of blissful lovemaking
cloud the truth. Nothing had changed. She and Jack had
very little in common. They were as different as espresso
coffee and beer. Heavens, if she'd been in Jack's shoes she
wouldn't have dreamed of staying back at the homestead
to play host to a stranger when she could have been taking
charge of the cattle muster.

When it came to the big things in life, they would always
make different choices, but man, oh, man, it was hard to
remember that when Jack was kissing her.

There'd actually been dangerous moments last night
when she'd almost wished she'd never started her pregnancy quest. But she couldn't think like that. It was wrong,

and she had to stay strong. She knew she'd made her decision carefully and for all the right reasons.

Jack wasn't on the phone for long. Lizzie was putting the kettle on, and when he came back into the kitchen the look on his face was rather puzzling. Lizzie couldn't tell if he was pleased or upset.

'That was Bill,' he said.

'Bill? The cook?'

'Yes.' With a wry smile, he came and stood beside her.

Lizzie caught a whiff of his aftershave and she had to fight an urge to lean in to him, to inhale the scent of the smooth, tanned skin above his shirt collar.

'So,' he said, standing so close that they were almost rubbing shoulders. 'Do you want the good news or the bad news?'

Bad news? Startled, she said, 'The good news, I guess.'

'You don't have to do any more cooking. Bill's coming back.'

She almost blurted out that she didn't mind cooking. She'd really been enjoying their meals, with just the two of them alone.

'Well,' she said, letting out a huff of surprise. 'I guess that'll give us both more time for our work.' Cautiously, she asked, 'So, what's the bad news?'

'I don't suppose it's actually bad news,' Jack said with an awkward smile. 'The men have finished the muster, and the team's coming back.'

'Back here?'

'Yes.'

'I see.' Lizzie was shocked by the slug of disappointment that hit her as she pictured Savannah teeming with cattlemen.

She'd become so used to being alone with Jack. Coming to Savannah had been like being shipwrecked on a desert island with a gorgeous man. Wasn't that every woman's fantasy? And wasn't it typical that she was only realising now how very much she'd enjoyed this time with him?

'The place will be swarming with people tomorrow,' Jack said, and he shot her a sharp glance. 'You know what this means, don't you?'

'I certainly wouldn't want to give any impression that we've been—um—close, Jack. I can't afford to have tongues wagging.'

He nodded and pulled a face. 'I thought you'd say that.'

'But you agree, don't you?' She felt a riff of panic. 'We don't want a scandal.'

Jack's mouth twisted as he grimaced. 'I'd hate to compromise you. Gossip spreads like wildfire in the bush. It's going to be bad enough when the men simply set eyes on you. They'll give me a ribbing, for sure, but, of course, I'll tell the Savannah ringers to pull their heads in.'

He let out an impatient sigh. 'Some of the team are contract workers. They'll be moving on from here, and who knows what they'll say? So, yeah, I agree we'll have to be careful.'

'Exactly,' Lizzie said sharply, but she was shocked to discover how miserable she was. Unreasonably so.

Jack reached for her hand, interlacing his fingers with hers, and, to her dismay, the simple contact made her feel warm and glowing, as if her insides were lit by something far deeper than lust.

'At least we have tonight,' he said in that easy, warmly persuasive way of his.

Oh, heavens. Was that wise? Minutes ago they'd been talking about her plans for the future. Jack wouldn't be a part of that future, but another night together would make their eventual break-up harder.

Perhaps the return of the ringers was a blessing in disguise. A wake-up call.

She looked down at Jack's hand, linked with hers. It was very workmanlike, broad and brown, and there was a pale, crescent-shaped, almost-healed scar on the knuckle of his thumb. This morning, this very hand had traced the letters of her name on the inside of her thighs.

The memory drugged Lizzie, making her hot and hollow, urging her to curl into Jack, to beg him to touch her again, there and everywhere, to cover her with kisses.

His thumb rubbed slowly along hers, silently seductive. When she looked up she could see the quiet certainty in his face, the barely contained desire.

When it came to longing, it seemed they were on the same page.

He slipped his arms around her shoulders, surrounding her with his strength, and the heat of his desire. Gently, he nuzzled her chin. 'We can't waste this one last night, Lizzie.'

With his arms around her and his lips roaming her throat, anything he said sounded perfectly reasonable.

The tide of longing rolled over her and she thought she might drown if she refused him. How could she spend this last night alone? What harm could there be in one more night with Jack?

One last, heavenly night, before her life went back to normal.

CHAPTER NINE

MIDNIGHT, and the moon shone so brightly it seemed to come right into bed with them. They were in Jack's bed, a symphony in grey, black and silver, and Lizzie lay on her side, so she could see him in the moonlight, amazed that she felt utterly at peace with herself and with the world.

Jack was a perfect lover and the loveliest man, and she didn't want to analyse this moment, or to try to justify in her head exactly why she was lying here with him. She just wanted to drink in the memory, to save it for the future…this feeling of perfect happiness and safety, of being in the right place, with the right man…at the right time…

Except…in the silver moonlight Jack's eyes were too shiny.

'Are you OK?' she whispered.

'Yes, of course.'

'You look sad.'

'Not sad, just thinking.'

'What about?'

He made a small sound of impatience, rolled onto his side, facing her, and lifted her fingers to his lips. He kissed them gently one by one. 'It's nothing,' he said. 'A bad memory. It's gone.'

Lizzie leaned closer, rubbed her lips over his jaw, loving the scratchiness of his beard. 'I hope you're feeling OK, because I'm feeling very OK. I might even be feeling a little bit smug.'

Jack smiled, and she was relieved to see that he looked more like his old self. 'So, I'm fine, and you're fine. How about Madeline?'

She laughed. 'Madeline's fine, too.' She settled her hand over the bump of her baby, which seemed to be growing incredibly fast. Almost immediately, to her utter astonishment, she felt a tiny flutter—a bumping motion under her hand.

'Jack!'

'What is it?'

Instantly he was up on one elbow, leaning over her, blocking the moonlight, so she couldn't see his face, but she thought she heard fear in his voice.

'It's OK. It's just the baby. I can feel her moving. She's kicking.'

'Yeah?' There was a shake in his voice, as if he was excited now. Or scared.

The little flutters inside her went on, making her think of the times she'd caught a moth in her hand and had felt its wings flapping against her palm.

'Here, you feel it.' Grabbing his hand, she pressed it against her. 'Can you feel that?'

'No,' he said. 'I can only feel you.' He let his hand slide over her skin. 'And you feel as silky and sexy as—'

He stopped, and then suddenly, ever so softly, 'Oh-h-h…'

'Can you feel it now?'

'Yes, I can…wow.'

'Isn't it the most amazing sensation?'

'She's certainly a cute little kicker. Better sign her up for the Moulin Rouge. Has she done this before?'

'I've never felt her before.'

'She's punching *and* kicking now,' Jack said.

'Is she? Let me have another feel.' Lizzie pushed her hand under Jack's and gasped when she felt two sets of tiny, bumping movements. 'She can't decide whether she wants to be a boxer or a soccer player,' she said.

'I wonder who she'll play for. Italy or Australia?'

Lizzie grinned happily into the moon-streaked darkness.

'I guess it depends on where you decide to live,' he said.

'Yes,' she agreed, aware that a sober note had crept into his voice.

After a bit, the baby quietened and Lizzie yawned and snuggled against him, not wanting to worry about the future.

It was lovely to lie here with Jack, just the two of them in the silent homestead, surrounded by the quiet outback night. Then she spoiled the peace by picturing Jack in the future, long after she was gone from here, sleeping in this house, in this bed perhaps, with his young, country bride.

'Oh, God, I wish—'

She cut off the words, horrified that she'd almost spoken her thoughts aloud.

'What?' Jack said. 'What do you wish?'

That I was ten years younger.

Lizzie shook her head, pressed her lips together to make sure the words couldn't escape.

'Come on, Lizzie. You tell me your wish, and I'll tell you mine.'

So he wished for something, too.

Lizzie remembered the shiny glitter in his eyes. Had they been tears?

This conversation was getting risky.

Sexual attraction was one thing. Sharing intimate wishes and dreams was another matter entirely. When physical intimacy included emotional intimacy, a casual affair became...

What?

What was the next step? Love?

Lizzie sat up abruptly, clutching the sheet over her breasts. 'The men might get back early. I should go back to my room now.'

'Don't. There's no need to go yet. They won't break camp until daybreak, and it'll take them half a day to travel back here.' Gently, Jack pulled her down beside him. 'Sleep here, Lizzie,' he said. 'No more talking. Just curl up and sleep.'

She was actually too tired to argue. Besides, sleeping was safe enough, and, when she considered the inviting curve of Jack's shoulder, Lizzie knew there was no nicer place to sleep.

Jack lay awake in the darkness with Lizzie's curves nestled against him. He could smell her hair, feel the gentle rise and fall of her breathing, and he wished this night might never end. When Lizzie was in his bed she was soft and womanly, and vulnerable and sweet. She was wild. She was his, and his alone.

In the morning she would retreat. Before the mustering team returned, she would tie her lovely hair into a tight knot and pull on her armour, like a crab shrinking back into its shell.

If he'd had his way, and if Lizzie had been any other woman, he would have spoken up tonight. He would have told her how he felt, how very much he wanted her, that he was pretty damn sure that he was falling in love with her. Then he would have told her. No, he would have *insisted* that there was no need to hide their feelings from outsiders.

Why should they give a damn what anyone else said or thought?

All very well for him, of course. He wasn't a federal senator. He'd never faced the press crying scandal because word of a liaison had leaked out. The only newspaper he'd been featured in was the Gidgee Springs freebie. Lizzie had come here in the first place to escape the press, so she had every right to call the tune.

No point in trying to change her mind…it would only ruin a perfect night.

Lizzie woke to the sound of a teacup rattling against a saucer. She opened her eyes to see Jack setting a cuppa on the table beside her.

'Good morning,' he said with a smile.

'Is that tea? How lovely. What time is it?'

'Half past seven.'

'Goodness, are the men here?'

'No, don't panic. I told you they won't be here for ages.'

She looked up at Jack shyly. He was already showered and dressed. 'Have you been up long?'

He shook his head.

'I slept very well.'

'I know.' Jack smiled and sat on the edge of the bed. 'I could hear you, all night long, snoring away.'

Lizzie stared at him, appalled. 'I don't snore.' Quickly she added, 'Do I?'

'Like a buzz saw.' Jack's right eyebrow hiked skywards. 'Hasn't anyone told you?'

'No.' Her voice was shrill with horror. 'It—it's been a while since I—' She bit her lip. 'Maybe it's the pregnancy.'

It was only then that she saw the mirth twinkling in his eyes.

'Hey,' she cried. 'You're pulling my leg again.'

'Only because you're so easy to tease.' He grinned as his hand fastened around her ankle through the bedclothes.

Lizzie rolled her eyes. Prim-mouthed, she reached for her cup of tea. 'Thanks for making this,' she said super-politely.

'Thank *you*, for last night,' Jack answered with soft emphasis.

'It was—' Lizzie discarded words like wonderful, and fabulous. She had to back off now. With the return of the stockmen, it was time to widen the emotional distance between them. She left the sentence dangling, and perhaps it was just as well, because suddenly her throat was choked with emotion.

Backing off and widening emotional gaps were all very well in theory, but they weren't very easy to put into practice. She liked Jack so much. Too much, and for all the right reasons.

Just sitting here, drinking a morning cuppa with him, felt like the nicest possible way to start the day.

I'm going to have to give him up, cold turkey, she thought, unhappily—*before I become hopelessly addicted*.

Jack broke into her thoughts. 'I should warn you—there'll be a slap-up dinner tonight for everyone. It's a tradition on Savannah. At the end of every big muster, we always put on a big dinner at the homestead for the whole team.'

'That's nice. Would it be best if I ate in my room?'

He looked surprised. 'No way. You're part of the household. You should be there. The guys will want to meet you.'

She managed a broken smile. It was the end of paradise. Setting down her teacup, she began to tidy her hair.

It was early afternoon when Jack heard the distant growl of a motor signalling that the mustering team was almost home. He went out onto the veranda, with Cobber at his heels. The dog's tail wagged and his nose twitched at the first scent of dust stirring on the horizon.

Together, man and dog watched the familiar cavalcade emerge out of the dust. First came the large mob of horses, then the truck with the gooseneck trailer carrying the stores and the kitchen. These were followed by the tray-back ute and a second trailer loaded with a trio of quad bikes.

This was the first time in years that Jack hadn't been part of the muster. For him, the big muster at the end of the wet season was one of the best things about his job. He always enjoyed being out there with the team, on the back of a sure-footed horse, dodging saplings and melon holes as he chased stragglers and cleanskins out of the thick scrub.

He loved camping out, too, yarning around the campfire at night with the men, sleeping under the stunning canopy of stars. This year, he'd fiercely resented Kate's request that he stay back at the homestead to play host to the lady senator.

It just showed that a man never knew the strange twists and turns his life might take. Now the appeal of the cattle muster was nothing compared with the hold Lizzie Green had on him.

Admittedly, Jack had never been one of those men, like many of his friends, who were totally wedded to the outback life. He knew guys who'd swear that there was no place on earth as good as this wide brown land, but those fellows had never really considered doing anything else. They'd gone away to boarding school for six years or so, and then they'd headed straight back to the bush.

More than once Jack had thought that he might have been happier, if he'd been like them. Knowing exactly where you belonged in this crazy world had to be a huge bonus. But he'd had his heart set on the Air Force and, once he'd known it was out of his reach, he'd returned to the outback as a second-best option.

Now he was setting his sights on another goal that was beyond his reach. Was he mad to feel so far gone over a high-flying woman from a different world? He knew deep down that he had little chance of a future with Lizzie, but the crazy thing was—he no longer seemed to have a choice.

She'd struck fire in his veins, and his life would never be the same again.

More than that—Jack knew now that it wasn't only his own happiness at stake. Deep in his bones, he was pretty damn sure he could make Lizzie happy, too. And her baby. Those two mightn't know it yet, but they needed him, no doubt about it.

He just had to find the best way to prove it.

'What do you want?' barked a voice in response to Lizzie's knock on the kitchen door.

'I was wondering if you'd like a hand.'

The man at the sink whirled around, and when he saw Lizzie his eyebrows rose high above his spectacles, his jaw dropped, and for a moment he seemed unable to speak.

She took a step into the kitchen and smiled. 'You must be Bill,' she said.

He nodded, shoved his glasses up his nose with a hand covered in soapsuds, and gave her a shaky smile.

'I'm Lizzie Green. I'm staying here, and Jack said you were putting on a big dinner tonight. I know he's busy, helping the men with the horses and everything. But I thought, after all the travelling and unpacking you've had to do, that you could probably use a spare pair of hands in here.'

'Well, that's mighty kind of you, miss—er—ma'am.'

'Lizzie,' she corrected, noting the remnants of his English accent.

Bill smiled shyly, showing a flash of gold in his front tooth, and he cast an anxious glance at the kitchen table, which was now almost sagging beneath the weight of unloaded camping supplies—half-used sacks of flour and sugar, bags of potatoes, tins of golden syrup, and bottles of sauce.

'So, what can I do?' Lizzie asked. 'What are you planning for dinner? I'm a dab hand at peeling potatoes.'

The cook swallowed his surprise and beamed at her, and she could tell she'd made a new friend.

The dinner was roast beef with Yorkshire pudding and roast vegetables and it was eaten in the big dining room that was hardly ever used.

Lizzie found a large white damask tablecloth and napkins in the linen press. They hadn't been ironed so she attended to that, and she found the good china and cutlery in the sideboard and had fun setting the table. She even went outside into the garden and found a few straggling daisies that made rather a nice centrepiece when combined with sprigs of purple bougainvillea.

At half past six, the men turned up on the veranda for pre-dinner drinks. They had showered and changed into clean clothes. Their riding boots were polished, and their hair was damp and carefully slicked back. They were all lean, wiry, sunburnt fellows, used to hard, physical work and unpractised in small talk.

Even so, while at first glance they seemed shy, when Jack introduced Lizzie they weren't fazed by the fact that she was a senator, and it wasn't difficult in the least to put them at their ease.

If she hadn't been pregnant, she would have had a beer with them. Instead, she accepted a glass of tonic water, and leaned back against a veranda post, asking only a few questions, happy to let the ringers talk about the weather and cattle, and the muster.

She rather liked the quiet, laconic manner of these men of the bush, and she thought how pleased she was to be gaining this insight into another aspect of Australian life.

Of course, she couldn't help noticing how disturbingly attractive Jack was by comparison. In a dark blue, long-sleeved shirt and cream chinos, he was the handsomest man in the group by a country mile. Across the veranda, she caught his eye, and for one heartbeat their gazes held, and she felt her skin grow hot.

Quickly, she looked down, hoping no one else had noticed her reaction. But she was sure she'd read approval in Jack's quiet smile, and she felt inordinately happy.

Jack would never have said as much, but he'd been uncertain about the likely success of the dinner party. The reserved outback men were bound to be a little star-struck about having a lady senator in their midst, and he wasn't sure if Lizzie would fit in.

He quickly realised that he shouldn't have worried. Lizzie put the men at ease straight away. Her clothes were right to start with—slim blue jeans and a dark red sweater with a simple V-neck that showed off the tiny gold cross— and she seemed to know exactly the right questions to ask, showing an interest in the men without being nosy.

Bill's enthusiasm for her was an unexpected bonus. The cook told everyone about Lizzie's help in the kitchen— another surprise for Jack. It seemed that, not only had she taken care of all the vegetables, but she'd helped stow away the provisions from the muster, *and* she'd got the dining room ready.

As the wine flowed so did the compliments from the men, corny or otherwise.

'Best peeled spuds I've ever tasted.'

'Better watch out, Cookie. You might lose your job.'

Fortunately, the men were sensitive enough to leave Lizzie's politics out of the conversation, so all in all the meal was relaxing and enjoyable for everyone.

It was all smooth sailing until one of the travelling contract musterers, a guy nicknamed Goat, dropped a clanger, out of the blue.

'I've seen a story about you,' he said to Lizzie. 'Saw it in a magazine down at the ringers' barracks.'

'Really?' Lizzie sounded cool enough, but Jack detected a nervous tilt to her smile. 'Which story was that?'

'Something in an old *Blokes Only*. I thought it was you and I checked it out before dinner.'

Jack stiffened, sensing trouble, then he saw the colour drain from Lizzie's face.

He forced himself to sound casual. 'Anything in that old mag is bound to be a lie.'

'Nice photo though,' Goat said, grinning stupidly. 'Would you like me to go and get it?'

'No!' Lizzie looked as if she might cry. 'I can't believe there are still copies of that around. It was years ago.'

'That's the bush for you,' chimed in Bill, clearly unaware of the undercurrents. 'People out here hang onto magazines for years, especially *Blokes Only*.'

'Anyway, it was all good,' said Goat. 'That old boyfriend of yours was full of praise. Said you were twelve on a scale of ten. In the sack, that is.'

'Goat!' Even Jack was surprised by the steely command

in his voice. Too bad. He was furious with the idiot. 'Pull your head in.'

Every head at the table turned to Jack. No one spoke.

His hands were tight fists, ready to slam the next mouth that let rip with a stupid comment. 'Show more respect to our guest,' he said coldly.

The men looked sheepish. Goat mumbled apologies.

Lizzie managed a brave smile. 'Has Jack told you that he jumped the stockyard gate?'

Jack's ears burned as attention turned to him, but he had to admire the skilful way Lizzie had deflected everyone's interest.

'What's this, Jack? You didn't take the round yard gate, did you?'

'With miles to spare,' Lizzie announced.

This was greeted by exclamations and cheers and thumping on the table.

Old Archie, the ringer who'd served the longest on Savannah, was grinning from ear to ear. 'Jeez, mate, you're a dark horse. When were you going to tell us?'

It took a while for the excitement to die down, but then Lizzie excused herself, saying she had to make an international phone call.

The men didn't talk about her again, at least, not in Jack's hearing, but he was pretty damn sure they'd be gawking at her in *Blokes Only* just as soon as they got back to their quarters. He couldn't believe how angry the thought made him.

Much later, when the men had gone and the house was in darkness, there was still a light showing under Lizzie's door.

Jack tapped lightly.

'Who is it?' she called.

'Me,' he said simply.

She came and opened the door just a chink. Her hair was loose to her shoulders and she was wearing a deep rose dressing gown, buttoned to the throat. Blocking the doorway, she stood with her arms crossed, eyes narrowed warily. 'How can I help you, Jack?'

'I just wanted to apologise for the way that fool carried on at dinner.'

'Thanks, but why should you apologise? It was hardly your fault.' She looked tired, with smudges of shadow beneath her eyes.

'I feel responsible,' Jack said. 'I knew how upset you were.'

She gave an exaggerated shrug. 'I'm OK. I'm used to it. The Iron Maiden Senator, remember?' With a glance down the darkened hallway, she said, 'Have they all gone?'

'Yes.'

She looked as if she planned to close her door. Jack said, quickly, 'Who spilled that story? It wasn't Mitch, was it?'

'No.' Lizzie closed her eyes, leaned back against the doorjamb. 'Even Mitch was above that. This time it was Toby.'

'Another boyfriend?'

She sighed wearily, slowly opened her eyes. 'Yes, the one I dated after Mitch. The successful banker I thought was serious. We'd been going together for twelve months, and we were unofficially engaged. I'd even started planning our family.'

A steel band tightened around Jack's chest. He wished he hadn't asked. He couldn't believe how much he hated hearing this, hated to think of Lizzie loving other guys, hated to see the bleak resignation in her eyes. But now she'd started, it seemed she needed to tell him the whole story.

'There'd been warnings,' she said. 'Photos of Toby in the

press with his arms around lovely models. He laughed it off. Said he'd been set up by the media and, like a fool, I believed him. Then I hardly heard from him for a month. He wasn't answering my calls. Suddenly the article in *Blokes Only* turned up. "Behind Closed doors with Senator Green".'

'How could you bear it?'

She tried to smile but her mouth wobbled. 'Not very well, especially when Toby admitted later that he'd done it partly because he knew I'd drop him. He hadn't been brave enough to tell me he wanted to break up.'

A groan broke from Jack.

'I toughed it out as usual,' she said, 'but it didn't do my career any good. I was about to chair a senate committee for family services. The story put an end to that.'

This time, her mouth turned square, and she really looked in danger of crying. She took a deep breath. 'So that's the story of Toby the toad. I'm going to bed. Goodnight, Jack.'

'Lizzie, I'm so sorry.'

He was talking to her closed door.

The next few days were particularly depressing for Lizzie. Not only because the whole business of Toby had been painful to relive, but because the recollections had made her see how very foolish she'd been to become romantically involved with Jack.

She'd sworn off men. She knew they always let her down, and yet once again she'd fallen.

But she wasn't only worried about her feelings; she was concerned about Jack too. When she remembered the genuine affection he'd shown to her, she felt a pang of guilt. She found herself thinking about her mother and father's affair.

Goodness, how could she have forgotten that salutary lesson?

Lisa Firenzi had enjoyed a holiday fling with Heath Green, a handsome, young Australian, and then she'd moved happily on without a backward glance. Not once had she stopped to consider that Heath might have been hurt by her love-him-and-leave-him attitude.

It wasn't until Lizzie had come to Australia many years later that she'd realised how deeply the affair had affected her father. He'd loved Lisa and he'd taken ages to get over losing her, and as a result he hadn't married until his late forties.

He was now very happily married to the widow of one of his best friends, and he was a very proud stepfather to her two sons...but he'd travelled through some very dark years.

Remembering again her father's pain, Lizzie left her desk and went to the doorway to look out at the long stretch of pale golden paddocks.

The more she thought about it, the more she knew she couldn't afford any more reckless moments with Jack. A casual affair rarely stayed casual, especially when the couple in question were living together, but there was no way she could expect her relationship with Jack to last beyond her stay at Savannah. It couldn't possibly work.

Jack belonged out here in the outback. How could she expect him to adapt to her lifestyle ruled by endless phone calls and meetings, interference from the media, cancelled holidays and interrupted meals? He would be much happier here, and he would make an amazingly fabulous husband for some lucky, *young* countrywoman.

He had all the right husbandly credentials. He might not be rolling in money, but he'd be a steady provider, good with children, caring and calm in an emergency. Throw in his good looks and his masterly bedding techniques and the man was a rare prize.

It couldn't be long at all before some smart girl snapped him up. And Jack would live happily ever after.

This, Lizzie told herself, was a very important reason why she must not mess up his life.

For heaven's sake, she'd chosen to have a sperm-donor baby so she could avoid awkward emotional entanglements. But from the moment she'd stepped from the plane on Savannah soil she'd been slipping under Jack's spell. The red outback dust had barely settled before the change had started.

But had she been terribly selfish?

CHAPTER TEN

Two mornings later, Jack gave up trying to stay away from Lizzie. He stuck his head through her doorway and found her sitting at her desk, concentrating as usual on her laptop screen, so he knocked.

Her eyes lit up with pleasure when she saw him, and his heart skipped like a day-old colt.

'How busy are you?' he asked.

'Why? Is something happening?'

'I thought you might like to get out of the office for a bit. We could go for a drive and I could show you the gorge.'

Her eyes widened. 'What gorge?'

'Porcupine Gorge. It's quite spectacular, and part of it runs through Savannah land.'

Frowning, she looked from him to her computer, then back to him again. The frown faded and colour rose in her cheeks. 'I must say this work on the Senate Appropriations Bill is very tedious. I'm very tempted to take a break.'

'Great,' Jack said, not giving her room for second thoughts. 'How long do you need to be ready?'

'Five minutes?'

He grinned, and Lizzie smiled back at him, her eyes

flashing with the glee of a schoolgirl released from a boring detention.

They set off, driving across the plains, and Jack was pleased that Lizzie seemed at ease and happy. She sat with the window down, not minding at all that her hair was being blown about.

He wished he felt as relaxed. He'd hated the silence between them and the subterfuge of this past week. He'd hated having to deny to every man and his dog that he was mad about Lizzie.

Pretending indifference was torture. Lizzie was in his thoughts first thing in the morning and last thing at night and most of the times in between. This whole charade was driving him insane.

And the men knew it, damn it.

Jack had sent Goat packing after one too many risqué suggestions, and he'd given the other men fleas in their ears over their nudge-nudge, wink-wink innuendoes.

But now he'd had enough of living the lie, which was why he needed to talk to Lizzie today. He'd always been a straight shooter, the kind of man who laid his cards on the table, then dealt with the consequences.

Today, however, the consequences were potentially huge. His relationship with Lizzie was at stake and he was sick with nerves.

Beside him, Lizzie had settled her hand on her belly, as if she was feeling the baby kick, and he had to ask, 'How's Madeline?'

She smiled shyly. 'She's turning into quite a gymnast. I'm amazed how active she is. I hate to think what she'll be like in a few months' time.'

He pictured Lizzie in the months ahead, wonderfully

ripe with pregnancy. She would be lovelier than ever, a beautiful, Madonna-like mother-to-be.

'I suppose all babies are active, whether they're girls or boys,' he said.

'I'm sure they must be.' Lizzie turned to him and frowned. 'Jack, you're not suggesting that Madeline might be a boy, are you?'

He grinned. 'I wouldn't dare.'

The frown lingered as she brooded over this. Eventually, she said, 'I can find out next week, if I want to.'

'What happens next week?'

'I have to go into Gidgee Springs for a check-up. There's a doctor who comes from Charters Towers once a month and he brings a portable ultrasound machine.'

'That's handy. I was wondering what you'd do about doctors.'

Lizzie patted her tummy. 'By next week, the baby should be big enough for the scan to pick up its sex, and I'll have to choose whether I want to know, or not.'

'Haven't you decided?'

She shook her head. 'I'm hopeless. One day, I'm absolutely positive I have to know straight away. The next, I don't want to know till it's born. I want to keep it as a surprise, the way it's always been for women all down the ages.'

'And for men,' Jack couldn't help adding.

Lizzie sent him a careful glance, as if she was trying to gauge his mood. 'I guess I'll make up my mind on the day of the ultrasound.'

'What day's that? I'll make sure I'm free to drive you into town.'

'Don't worry. I can just borrow a vehicle.'

'No, you won't, Lizzie. I'm not letting you drive all that way on your own.'

'Well…thank you,' she said quietly. 'My appointment's next Wednesday.'

As they continued on across the grassy plains, the sun climbed higher and the autumn mists melted, leaving the air as crisp and sparkling as champagne. Lizzie watched a pretty flock of galahs take off in front of them, filling the sky with a fluttering mass of soft grey wings and rosy pink breasts.

She thought how familiar the landscape seemed now after only a short time on Savannah. She doubted it could ever feel like home for her, but she was beginning to understand why people like Kate Burton and Jack could live here quite happily for most of their lives.

Jack parked the ute in the sparse shade of a gum tree, but Lizzie, peering through the windscreen, saw nothing but plains ahead.

'Where's the gorge?'

'We need to walk the last little bit.'

With Cobber following, tail wagging madly, they left the vehicle and strolled across red earth dotted with occasional trees and pale, biscuit-coloured clumps of grass. The ground gradually became stonier and eventually turned to rock.

And then, in front of them, the ground disappeared completely, dropping away into a deep, wide ravine.

Lizzie took a cautious step forward. 'Oh, dear.' A wave of dizziness washed over her, and she swayed precariously.

'Whoa.' Instantly, Jack pulled her back into the safety of his arms. 'Careful.'

'I'm afraid I don't have a very good head for heights.'

'Come away from the edge, then.' He drew her further back, keeping an arm about her.

'It's OK now. I want to see it, and I'm starting to feel better.' Especially now that Jack's arms were around her.

She allowed herself to sink back against the solid wall

of his chest, and she closed her eyes, savouring the wonderful sense of sanctuary he gave her.

Jack, lovely Jack.

Carefully, she opened her eyes again, and discovered that she could look down at the sheer fall of the red cliffs and the narrow ribbon of the river way down below without feeling faint. 'You're right,' she said. 'It's spectacular.'

As his strong arms encircled her he pressed a kiss to the side of her neck, and she could smell the special spiciness of his aftershave.

The warm pressure of his lips was unbearably sweet on her skin, and she very nearly made the mistake of leaning her head to one side, in an open invitation for Jack to kiss her neck and her throat.

Just in time she remembered that this shouldn't be happening.

Oh, good grief. Oh, help.

Damn. She'd promised herself she would be strong.

'Jack.'

His arms tightened around her and he murmured something dreamily incomprehensible against her neck.

'Jack, you mustn't…we shouldn't…'

'Of course we should.' His lips continued their mesmerising journey over her skin, and she loved it.

Oh, heavens, she adored it. But she'd spent a week telling herself that she mustn't let this happen. She was older than Jack and supposedly wiser. It was up to her to call a halt. She had to; she must.

'Jack, no!'

It came out too loudly, so loudly that he couldn't mistake her command. He let his hands drop and he stepped away.

Crossing her arms over her front, Lizzie felt cold shivers chase each other over her skin. She'd wanted to be in his arms, wanted his kisses…wanted his touch…wanted everything…

But to let things continue could only be selfish. She took several deep breaths as she struggled to think calmly and clearly.

Jack was standing with his legs spread, hands hanging loosely at his sides, jaw clenched, green eyes unhappy. Wary.

Lizzie tried to smile and failed. Their morning was already spoiled and it was her fault. 'I'm sorry, Jack.'

After the longest time, he said, quietly, *too* quietly, 'I've brought picnic things. Why don't you sit on this log, while I fetch them?'

She was startled by the change in him. She'd expected sparks and anger laced with charm, not this quiet, contained politeness. Sinking onto the broad, silvery log of a fallen river gum, she watched Jack go without another word back to the ute, with Cobber following.

He brought a woven cane picnic basket, a tartan rug and a blackened billycan, which he set on one end of the log, before he scouted around for dried leaves, twigs and branches for a fire.

'Can't have a picnic in the bush without boiling a billy of tea,' he said, without smiling.

'No, I guess not.' She couldn't help admiring the picture Jack made, crouched beside the fire, feeding in sticks, then lighting the match and holding it for a moment between his cupped hands, letting the flame burn steadily before carefully setting it to the dry leaves.

She was trying very hard to push aside memories of those same strong, capable hands making love to her. She concentrated very hard on the first wisps of smoke, then the red flames appearing, flickering and crackling. She caught the unique eucalyptus scent of scorched gum leaves and very soon the kindling blackened, then turned to ash, while the larger wood burned.

Jack set the billy in the middle of the fire, and she was relieved to see that he was almost back to normal. He'd always been so very good-humoured; it was disconcerting to see him upset.

Just the same, they had to talk. They couldn't go on without settling things. It was important that they both agreed their romance didn't have a future. Friendship was a much saner option.

When the tea was ready, Jack spread the rug on shaded grass with a fabulous and less scary view of the gorge. Sprawled comfortably in the dappled shade of an ironbark, they drank from tin mugs and ate biscuits.

Lizzie broke a biscuit in half. 'Is Cobber allowed one?'

Jack shrugged. 'Sure.'

She tossed it, and Cobber caught it in mid-air, downing it in one blissful, doggy gulp. She laughed, then quickly sobered. She mustn't put this off any longer.

'Jack, I'm sorry about…what happened before. I overreacted.'

He looked away, fixing his attention on a windblown tree that clung precariously to the edge of the opposite cliff. 'I guess it was bad timing.'

'I'm afraid it's not as simple as timing.'

His gaze snapped back to her. 'What do you mean?'

When he looked at her with those beautiful, challenging green eyes, Lizzie wanted to give in, to admit that resistance was beyond her.

Heavens, she had to be stronger than this. 'I'm sure you understand that we can't continue…the way we were…'

A muscle in his jaw jerked hard, and he sat up, abruptly. 'We could if we were prepared to be honest. It's crazy to try to hide how we feel.' He shot her a sharp glance. 'The men have guessed anyhow.'

'But if we're honest, what exactly can we tell them, Jack? That we've had a fling?'

'*Had* a fling?' He stared at her for long, painful seconds. 'You're talking in the past tense.'

'I know. Because—' Lizzie swallowed painfully '—I don't see how it can be anything else.'

More silence, longer and more painful than the last. Jack's unhappy eyes searched her face. 'What are you going to tell me next, Lizzie? That we both knew our relationship was going nowhere?'

Yes, this was exactly what she needed to tell Jack, but they were the very words Mitch had used all those years ago. Had Jack remembered?

Pinching the bridge of her nose, she tried to hold back the tears that threatened, tried to think sensibly. 'You know we can't have a long-term relationship, Jack.'

'I don't know that at all. Why can't we? I'd be happy to go back to Canberra with you.'

'No.'

'Why not?'

'You'd hate it. I know you would. You don't understand what my life's like. All the meetings. The pressure. Living out here is a holiday by comparison.' Despairing, Lizzie shook her head. 'Jack, we have to get this into perspective.'

She blinked, took a breath. 'We're a man and a woman, who suddenly found each other, and we were totally alone, with complete privacy, and there was…an attraction.'

'There's still an attraction.'

'Well, yes,' she admitted. At least she owed him that much honesty. 'But we both knew from the start that we couldn't have a future together.'

'We both knew?' he repeated coldly.

'Yes! For heaven's sake, Jack. You're a thirty-year-old man. You knew that I'm ten years older than you. You knew that I'm pregnant with a child that's not yours. You knew about my career and that I'm only here for a short stay.'

Jack merely smiled into the distance. 'Is that list supposed to scare me off?'

'I would have thought so, yes.'

Slowly he brought his gaze back to her, and it was so hard, so unlike the Jack she knew, she began to tremble.

'What if I told you that not one of those things bothers me, Lizzie? I don't give a fig about your age. You're you.' His eyes shimmered, turning her skin to goose bumps. 'You're a beautiful and gutsy woman. I could give you a list of qualities that's as long as your arm. Your age doesn't come into it.'

Oh, Jack. Any minute now she was going to spoil everything by bursting into tears. 'Jack—'

He silenced her with a glare. 'No matter what you say, I'm damn sure that baby of yours could benefit from having a father around. As for going back to the city to continue your work—' His shoulders lifted in a sudden shrug. 'I'm not tied to the bush.'

'But you've lived here all your life.'

'So what? This place doesn't define me.' With a wave of his hand he dismissed the gorge, the grassy plains, the bright blue sky. 'I'm here by default. My plan, when I was growing up, was to join the RAAF, as a fighter pilot.'

'A fighter pilot?' She couldn't hide her astonishment.

'It was all I ever wanted. I had no plans to stay in the outback. I worked my butt off to escape, to get away from here, and I made sure I had all the qualifications, the skills.'

Shocked, she tried to picture this alternative version of Jack. 'What happened?'

His mouth twisted in a bitter smile. 'I failed the psych test. Didn't have the vital mix of aggression and cockiness. I'd seen too much of that in my old man, and I couldn't pump my ego to the level they needed.'

This made perfect sense to Lizzie. Of course, Jack didn't have a killer instinct. Even so, she could feel the pain of his youthful disappointment, and her heart ached for him.

'But if you went to the city now, what would you do?'

'I have a few ideas. Business plans.'

Lizzie found herself entranced by this idea. 'Bill told me you've a great head for business. He said you do amazing calculations in your head, and you have a nose for the stock market.'

Jack frowned. 'When were you talking to Bill?'

'While we were working together in the kitchen.'

He shrugged. 'I've looked after my finances and I've made some successful investments. I don't want to make the same mistakes my old man made.'

She almost allowed herself to be swept away by the thought of Jack in the city, by her side, running his own business, and helping her to bring up her child. It seemed perfect. Too good to be true.

It *was* too good to be true.

Too soon the bubble burst, and Lizzie could see the real picture—the inevitable journalists swarming around them. The headlines about Jack, the photos, the questions.

Are you the reason Senator Green went into hiding? How do you feel about her sperm-donor baby? How old are you, Jack? Who do you vote for? Why aren't you the baby's father? Are you sterile?

Oh, heavens. She couldn't put him through that. It would be horrendous. He'd hate it. It couldn't work. She couldn't believe he would be happy.

And how could she take such a risk with *her* own happiness?

Twice before she'd fallen deeply in love—and she'd promised herself that she wouldn't line up for an agonising third bout of heartache. Not now, not with her baby coming.

She had to break up with Jack. Now. Cleanly and quickly. Not like the cowards, Mitch and Toby, who'd been too scared to face her. Their spinelessness had hurt her even more than losing them.

Straightening her shoulders, Lizzie turned to Jack, and her heart hurt as if it held splinters of glass. 'You know it can't work for us, Jack. I've told you why I settled on a sperm-donor baby, why I plan to live as a single mother.'

A muscle twitched in his jaw. 'Because you won't risk getting involved again.'

'Yes, that's part of my reason.' If only he didn't look so unhappy. 'But this isn't just about me. I'm trying to think about your happiness, too. You're a fabulous catch for any woman—any *young* woman, that is—and there must be oodles of girls, closer to your age, who'd snap you up in a heartbeat.'

Her brave admission was greeted by silence and she was left to stare, through a blur of tears, at the long, never-ending stretch of flat plains and the cloudless blue dome of the sky overhead. She knew the age difference was a poor excuse. Jack had a natural maturity that set him head and shoulders above men much older than him.

Hoping Jack couldn't see, she lifted her hand to dash the tears away. Then she heard his voice.

'Just think about one thing, Lizzie. Ask yourself if you were making love.' He spoke quietly and coldly, so unlike himself. 'Or were you just having meaningless sex?'

Without waiting for her response, he stood and began to stamp out the embers of their fire.

As they drove back to the homestead their chilled silence filled the ute's cabin. Lizzie wished she could think of something helpful to say. She wondered if she should offer to leave Savannah immediately, and she was shocked by how wretched that possibility made her feel.

When at last they drove through Savannah's gates she turned to Jack. 'Thanks for showing me the gorge.'

'My pleasure,' he said in his driest tone.

'About next week, Jack, when I go to the doctor, I'd be happy to drive into—'

Her words were cut off as he slammed on the brakes.

'You're not going to drive into Gidgee Springs. I won't allow it.'

'But it's a sealed road.'

'Lizzie, for crying out loud.' His hand thumped the steering wheel. 'It's over a hundred kilometres of bush, and there are no shops, no garages. No nice policeman to come to your rescue if you have a flat tyre. You'll be stranded.'

She knew that his anger was fuelled as much by their break-up as his concern for her driving safety. It was scary to know she'd pushed easy-going, sanguine Jack to the limits of his self-control.

'I'll take you in,' he said stiffly.

'Thank you,' she said, suitably chastened. 'That's very kind.'

Outwardly as calm as the quiet, copper-tinted afternoon, Jack stood at the horse-paddock fence, elbows on the weathered timber rail, while he inwardly wrestled with Lizzie's low blow.

He'd been through the gamut of emotions today. First he'd been angry at the way he'd stuffed up, rushing everything—the kiss, the conversation, the whole catastrophe. Hell, Lizzie had gone to the gorge expecting a pleasant diversion from her work. Instead, he'd put the hard word on her.

He hadn't told her nearly enough of the things he'd meant to say, about how important she was to him, how she made him feel, how special she was, the hundred reasons he was mad about her.

He'd returned, sunk in disappointment and despair. But now, at last, he was beginning to feel calmer, and he knew he wasn't going to throw in the towel. Not yet. There was no point in simply giving up, the way he had when he was a kid after he'd lost his career dreams.

No doubt Lizzie was expecting him to take her rejection sweetly on the chin and walk away without a fight. Laid-back Jack, easy to like, easy to let go.

Not so, sweetheart.

The woman had no idea how much he wanted her. Or why.

Truth to tell, Jack had asked himself that question many times this afternoon, running again through the list of negatives Lizzie had rattled off.

Why her? Why a politician? Why a forty-year-old? Why a woman who was pregnant with another man's child?

The more he thought about it, the more he was certain of his answers. To start with, he knew for sure that the overwhelming feelings he had for Lizzie weren't merely about her superb good looks. Lizzie was different, unique. Special. If she were eighteen or fifty, she would still be the woman he wanted.

Little things made him wild about her. The way she could turn to look at him and smile, tilting the left-hand side of her mouth more than the right. And then there was the gliding way she walked, and the way she carried herself like a proud princess, with her head high, shoulders back.

Lizzie had presence. She was smart. He totally understood why her political party had grabbed her. She was one classy woman.

But the biggest thing, damn it, the overwhelming reason Jack couldn't let Lizzie go was the dazzling chemistry between them. He'd sooner lose an arm than let *that* die.

Not that he had a clue how to win her back.

Only one thing was certain. It wasn't going to happen until she realised that she needed him. She did need him. Jack was sure of that—and Lizzie was too clever to overlook the truth—but it meant he had no choice but to be patient.

Sadly, patience was not his strongest virtue.

Over the next few days, Lizzie found Jack to be polite and friendly and distant, a perfect gentleman who treated her like a visiting lady senator. He respected her privacy, he ensured she had every creature comfort, and, in response to her questions, he courteously provided any amount of general information about the running of a cattle property.

She hated every minute of it.

She wanted the old Jack, the cheeky, cheerful Jack. Most of all, she wanted to see that intriguing, devilish sparkle in his eyes.

It was very alarming to discover that she was utterly two-faced. She'd told Jack flatly that their affair was over, and then, immediately, she was dying for it to resume. Her integrity seemed to have deserted her.

The worst of it was that, instead of feeling calm and relieved, she was more distracted than ever, unable to concentrate on her work, or her reading. Most nights, she reached for her book about single mothers and their babies, in the hope that it might clear her mind of Jack.

By the light of her reading lamp, she looked again at the photographs of women who'd become single mothers by choice. Giving birth, bathing babies, breastfeeding, cheering their babies on as they learned to crawl, or to place one block precariously on top of another.

Each charming photo was glowing evidence that a mother and her baby could be perfectly happy and a complete unit. Alone. Just the two of them, the way she'd planned when she'd first embarked on her pregnancy project.

The photos were supposed to help, but each night when Lizzie turned out the light and tried to sleep the only picture in her head was Jack.

She was beginning to think she had no choice but to leave Savannah sooner than planned—thank Kate kindly, but admit that the experiment hadn't worked—then return south, to face the music.

Alone.

On the morning of the doctor's appointment, Lizzie woke up feeling quite butterflies-in-her-stomach nervous.

Jack was taking her to town in Savannah's best vehicle, an air-conditioned four-wheel drive, and he had it waiting at the bottom of the front steps, promptly as she'd requested, just before nine o'clock.

When she came down the steps he strode around the front of the car, opened the passenger door, and greeted her with a frown. 'First time I've seen you in a dress.'

'I thought I'd better make an effort seeing as I'm going to town.'

'Gidgee Springs is not exactly Queen Street.'

'I'm not overdressed, am I?'

The look in Jack's eyes brought a lump to her throat. 'You're perfect.'

They drove out along the track that wound across the paddocks, stopping to open and close gates—Lizzie was now an expert—then onto a long, flat blue ribbon of bitumen.

'By the way, I've decided I want to find out,' she said.

His eyebrows rose. 'Whether Madeline's a boy or a girl?'

'Yes. After all, I'm having a very twenty-first-century pregnancy, and it makes sense to take advantage of all available information.'

He nodded. 'It's a red-letter day, then.'

'Yes, I'm pretty excited.' *And nervous.* She wouldn't tell him that. 'What will you do while I'm at the doctor's?'

'Oh—' He shrugged elaborately. 'I'll be busy. There's always plenty of business to see to when I'm in town.' He shot her a sharp glance. 'Unless you'd like someone there. For support.'

Her heart did a weird little jig at the thought of Jack sharing such a momentous experience, but she couldn't use him like that. For days she'd been feeling ashamed that she'd been the one to initiate their lovemaking. Jack was right to have asked about her motives. Looking back, it seemed terribly selfish. She couldn't lean on him any more.

'Thanks,' she said. 'That's a very kind offer, but I'll be all right.'

The visiting doctor from Charters Towers smiled at Lizzie. 'Now, if you'll just hop up onto this table, we'll check your baby's progress with the ultrasound.'

So this was it. The moment of truth. As Lizzie tried to make herself comfortable on the hard narrow bench she felt flutters of panic, and she wished that Jack were there beside her.

He'd been doggedly cheerful and perfunctory when he'd dropped her off at the doctor's surgery, saying that he'd be back in half an hour. While she was here, having her scan, he would be dashing around Gidgee Springs on business—calling at the saddler's, at the hardware store, at the bank, and the stock and station agency.

Once Lizzie was finished with the doctor, she was to join Jack at the Currawong café to try their famous hamburgers before they headed back to Savannah.

Their plan had all sounded exceedingly straightforward and sensible. Until now.

Now, on the very brink of discovering her baby's sex, the moment felt suddenly too big to experience on her own. Which was pretty silly considering there'd been no one besides the doctor when she'd been artificially inseminated, or when she'd been told she was pregnant.

She tried to cheer herself up by imagining Jack's reaction when she told him about the baby at lunchtime.

'All set?' the doctor enquired.

Lizzie nodded, and concentrated on slow, calming breaths as he applied cold gel to her abdomen. She'd never liked medical procedures, and she could never make sense of the black and white shapes on the ultrasound screen, so she closed her eyes, letting the doctor do his job, while she tried to relax.

Think yoga. You're drifting on a cloud...

She felt the probe sliding over her skin, and she remembered the dream she'd had about her baby—a perfect tiny girl curled inside her. The dream had been so very reassuring. All was well. She clung to the memory now.

The probe moved on, stopping every so often while the machine made clicks and beeping sounds.

'Well, well,' said the doctor suddenly.

Lizzie's eyes flashed open. She saw the surprise in the doctor's eyes and her relaxation evaporated. 'What is it? Is something wrong?'

CHAPTER ELEVEN

JACK chose a booth near the window in the Currawong café, so that he had a clear view across the street to the doctor's surgery. He couldn't believe how nervous he was, how much he cared about Lizzie and this baby of hers.

When the surgery door opened and Lizzie appeared, his heart gave a painful thud.

She looked beautiful, dressed for town in a sleeveless, aqua-blue dress, bare-legged and wearing sandals of woven brown and gold leather. His eyes feasted on her as she crossed the street, hips swaying seductively. She'd left her hair down for once, and it flowed about her shoulders as she moved, shining in the sunlight, dark as a raven's wing.

She reached the footpath and looked towards the café, and that was when Jack saw that her face was too pale and her eyes were glazed with shock.

Instantly, he was on his feet, his chair scraping the tiles, his heart knocking against the wall of his chest.

The doctor had given her bad news. There could be no other explanation. A rock the size of a tennis ball lodged in his throat. His fists curled tightly as he steeled himself to be strong. For Lizzie's sake.

He loved her.

As he watched her come through the café doorway he could no longer avoid the truth. If Lizzie had bad news, it was his bad news. He would do anything for her, would go anywhere in the world, work at whatever he could find, take on whatever role she wanted.

To his eternal shame, he also felt a glimmer of hope. Surely now she must know that she needed him.

Lizzie's mind was still reeling as she entered the café. She saw Jack standing at the table by the window, saw him wave and smile, and he looked so handsome and familiar and dear she could have kissed him.

She might have kissed him if the group of countrywomen at a nearby table hadn't all stopped talking and turned to stare at her. Lizzie gave them a nod and a scant smile, and she could feel their eyes following her as she made her way to Jack.

'You look as if you need to sit down,' he said, solicitously pulling out a chair for her.

'Thank you.'

Her shoulder brushed his arm as she sat, and she caught a comforting whiff of his familiar scent and his laundered shirt. He resumed his seat and looked at her with a complicated expression of tenderness and concern.

Tears threatened. Lizzie took a deep breath and willed them away.

Jack had ordered a pot of tea but it sat, untouched, between them along with the requisite cups and saucers, small milk jug, sugar bowl and tea strainer.

'How did it go?' he asked. 'Are you OK?'

Was she? She felt strangely numb. It was the shock, she supposed. 'It didn't go quite as I expected.'

Jack swallowed. 'Is there something wrong?' He repeated his first question. 'Are you OK?'

'Yes. I'm fine. Fit as a healthy horse.'

Lizzie sent a hasty glance over her shoulder and caught several women at the other table watching her from behind their teacups.

Leaning across the table to Jack, she lowered her voice. 'But I'm afraid there's not going to be any Madeline.'

'What's happened?' he whispered, and he looked understandably worried. 'You're still pregnant, aren't you?'

'Oh, yes. I'm most definitely pregnant.' It was hard to talk about this in whispers.

After a puzzled moment, Jack said, 'Does that mean you're having a boy?'

Lizzie nodded. 'But not just one boy.'

For a moment he simply stared at her, and then his brow cleared and his face broke into an incredulous grin. 'Twins?'

A nervous laugh escaped her. 'Twin boys. Can you believe it?'

The café fell silent. Too silent, Lizzie realised. Had she raised her voice?

'That's fabulous, Lizzie.' Reaching across the table, Jack gripped her hand. 'But I think we should find somewhere else to have this conversation, don't you?'

'Yes, please.'

'I've ordered our hamburgers. I'll tell them we want to take them away and we can find somewhere for a picnic.'

'Good idea.'

Avoiding the curious glances of the other customers, Lizzie went to the counter with Jack, where he paid for their tea and burgers and bought two bottles of lemon mineral water. Then they left quickly, escaping into the dusty, almost empty main street of Gidgee Springs.

Outside, Jack turned to her, grinning madly, clearly excited. 'Twin boys. Wow! That's amazing. Congratulations.' He gave her a one-armed hug. 'Aren't you pleased?'

'I don't know.' It was all Lizzie could honestly say. She still couldn't quite believe she was having twin boys. Two big, bouncing boys, the doctor had said. She knew she should be pleased. In time she was sure she'd be pleased, but she'd had her heart set on one manageable little girl.

Balancing her career with one baby, whether it was a boy or a girl, had always seemed doable. But twins? Twin boys? Even with a nanny, how on earth would she cope with raising two boys on her own?

'Here's our car,' Jack was saying, and Lizzie dragged her mind back to the present. 'I suggest we drive to Emu Crossing.'

'Is it far?'

'Five kilometres. There's a nice spot on the creek bank for a picnic.' Jack smiled. 'You can get over your shock without half the town watching.'

'I'd appreciate that. Thank you.'

As they drove out of town Lizzie watched the passing scenery in a kind of daze. Dimly, she was aware that everything about her seemed normal—vivid blue skies, ochre-red earth, white-trunked gum trees and grass the colour of pale champagne—but her head was buzzing with the idea of twins. Twin boys.

Double the trouble.

What on earth did she know about boys?

She had friends with sons, of course. From what she'd observed, little boys played endless soccer and cricket, and one or two of them had kept frogs in their pockets. Others had spent hours in the backyard—*heavens, my apartment doesn't even have a backyard*—playing with their dogs until they were covered in mud and came inside smelling like puppies.

Their mothers adored them, of course, so Lizzie was sure she would adore her boys, too.

Just the same, the idea of having two of them was overwhelming. Two rowdy and messy boys instead of one tidy and quiet girl. Perhaps it was some kind of cosmic joke?

Out of the blue, a new question arrived. Would the boys look like their father?

For the first time, she wished she knew more about donor number 372. What would it be like for boys to grow up without knowing him?

Then she remembered, with a bigger shock, that history was repeating itself. Her family would have another set of twin boys to follow on from Alessandro and Angelo. Another generation.

It was a sobering thought on all kinds of levels, and now, thinking again about the whole sorry business between her mother and Luca, Lizzie made an instant decision. She wouldn't let her little boys down. Whether she stayed in politics or found another job, she would do everything in her power to give her sons the very best start in life.

Encouraged by this resolution, she sent Jack a smile. 'I think I'm slowly starting to adjust to the news.'

'Good for you.'

'I just have to wrap my head around the idea that I'll be bringing up two boys.'

'It'll be interesting.'

Jack slowed down, then turned off the main road, disrupting a flock of grazing budgerigars that took off in a wild fluttering of bright green and yellow.

Ahead of them now lay a perfect picnic spot—a grassy bank overlooking a creek lined with majestic paperbarks that leant out over the wide, still water, as if they were admiring their reflections. Close to sandy shallows a lone white heron waded silently, patiently.

Jack threw down the tartan rug, and when Lizzie was comfortable he handed her a hamburger. 'Better tuck into these before they get soggy.'

Fortunately, the burgers weren't the least bit soggy. Lizzie licked her lips. 'This is so good. I hadn't realised I was hungry.'

'You're eating for three,' Jack said, smiling, and then he raised his drink bottle. 'Anyway, here's to your news.'

'It is good news, isn't it?'

'Of course it is. The best.' Slowly his grin faded and his expression grew serious. 'Do you think two boys will bring the father into the equation?'

Lizzie felt her cheeks grow hot. 'How do you mean?'

Jack shrugged. 'I know it's a long way off, but I was thinking that your boys will eventually want to know who their father is.'

'Oh.' Her stomach churned uncomfortably. 'I suppose it's more than likely that they'll want to make contact with him when they're older. They can do that now, when they're eighteen.'

'So your six-feet-three engineer could be a busy man.'

'Why?'

'He could have fifty or more kids trying to track him down.'

Lizzie winced. 'I—I suppose that's possible.' She hadn't allowed herself to think too much about the other babies her donor might have fathered.

'Eighteen years is a long time, Lizzie. Your sons will be adults by then, and in the meantime they won't have a male role model.'

'I'm aware of that,' she said tightly. 'But I grew up without a father, and I wasn't harmed.'

'But as soon as you were old enough, you came to Australia to be with your dad. And I imagine he welcomed you with open arms.'

Too true. Would her boys be so lucky? A sudden, painful ache burned in Lizzie's throat. Her eyes stung, and her appetite was ruined.

She dropped the last of her hamburger back into the paper bag, and leaned forward, hugging her knees, remembering her tempestuous teens, and her growing need to come to Australia to get to know her father. She could still remember exactly how she'd felt when she'd hurried from the plane at Sydney airport.

She would never forget that spine-tingling moment when she'd seen her dad, and the way his eyes had glittered with tears, and how he'd hugged her, so tightly she couldn't breathe.

He'd taken her to his flat near Sydney Harbour and they'd sat on the balcony overlooking the water, arms linked, talking and talking for hours and hours and hours.

The next day he'd taken her sailing, teaching her the ropes with gentle patience, and she'd felt as if she'd truly come home.

The memories brought goose bumps out on her arms, which only grew worse when she projected forward, and imagined her boys in their teens. Teenage boys were always a worry. More often than not they were angry about something, no matter how carefully they were raised. How would her boys feel about the unusual circumstances of their birth?

Had she made a terrible mistake, trying to do this alone? For so long she'd put her career first, but then she'd wanted a baby so much, and she'd planned to be both mother and father, but it wasn't possible, was it?

She stole a glance at Jack. He was, of course, perfect father material—warm and loving and full of fun, manly and athletic, tough without being rough. Her little boys would adore him.

She would adore him.

A hot tear fell onto her hand. Aghast, she tried to dash it away without Jack noticing.

Jack noticed.

He saw the way Lizzie's hands tightened around her knees, and he watched her chin tremble. Then, oh, God, a silver tear slid down her cheek.

It was too much. He couldn't stay away a second longer.

'Hey.' Leaning forward, he drew her gently into his arms. 'Hey, Lizzie… Lizzie.'

He couldn't bear to see her crying, but, if she needed to cry, this was how it had to happen. On his shoulder. In his arms. She might not have worked it out yet, but this was where she belonged. He loved her, and she needed him. The certainty of that was not fading.

'I'm sorry,' she sobbed, pressing her hot face against his neck.

'It's OK.' Jack stroked her silky, fragrant hair. 'You've been under too much pressure.'

For sweet seconds, she clung to him with a kind of desperation, but then, abruptly, she lifted her head, and took several deep breaths. 'I don't want to cry. I'm not really sad.'

'Just stressed,' he suggested.

'Yes.' Offering a watery smile, she touched her fingertips to his jaw. 'Thank you.'

He captured her hand in his. 'Lizzie, you've got to let me help you.'

'You have helped me, Jack. You've been…perfect. I'm really grateful.'

'I want to go on helping you.' His heart began a fretful pounding. 'If you give me a chance, Lizzie, I won't let you down.'

'It's too much to ask of you. I'm leaving here, Jack. And I'm forty, and I'm about to get huge and give birth to two babies and—'

'And I don't care. Honestly, Lizzie, none of those things bother me. Can't you believe that?'

Lizzie shook her head, as Jack knew she would, but he could no more remain silent than fly to the moon. 'I love you, Lizzie, and I want the whole package. To be a part of your life. I mean it. I love you.'

Her hazel eyes filled with tears and Jack felt his heart drop from a great height.

'Don't say that,' she whispered. 'You mustn't.'

'But it's the truth. I've been falling in love with you from the moment you stepped down from that plane. I'm mad about you, Lizzie. There's so much I want to do for you. Your life is so hard and it's going to get harder and you're trying to do it all on your own. I know you need me. And your boys are going to need me.'

'Oh, Jack.' Her face twisted miserably as she pulled her hands from his. She scrambled to her feet. Jack followed.

'Can't you understand?' she cried. 'I can't turn to you now, simply because my life's getting difficult. I've already worried myself sick because it looks as if I've simply used you. I don't want to make it worse by asking you to help me now, because I'm expecting twin boys. I'd really feel I was exploiting you.'

'Exploiting me? Are you crazy? You're the best thing that's ever happened to me.'

With a frantic shake of her head, she looked away, down the creek. 'I've been thinking for days now that I've imposed on you for too long. I know you feel sorry for me now, but it's time I left Savannah. I want you to get your life back to normal.'

'Back to normal. Hell, Lizzie!' He gave a wild laugh. 'Back to normal would be taking you back to my bed.'

Her response was a soft, sad little cry, half groan, half sob, and she seemed to sway on her feet as she closed her eyes.

Jack stared at her lowered lashes, at her quivering mouth, so lush and sexy, even though it was distorted by her effort not to cry. Without the slightest hesitation he stepped forward, wrapped her in his arms and kissed her.

And he delivered a message Lizzie couldn't miss.

Oh, heavens. Lizzie was full of great intentions. From the first, she tried to resist Jack's kiss. She stiffened the moment his lips touched hers, but then his arms tightened around her, and she was enveloped by the smell of sunlight on his skin...and then his tongue touched hers, and she was clinging to him, and she couldn't remember how to resist. Or why it was necessary.

Her protests were swept away by whispers in her head that Jack loved her, loved her, loved her...and by blissful sensations...and soaring happiness...

Until he finally released her.

Only then did she hear the ripple of wind on the water and in the trees. She felt its coolness on her skin, and she came, panting and breathless, to her senses.

Quickly, she regathered her wits, and her armour. 'That kiss wasn't very helpful, Jack.'

His eyes glittered with a knowing green light. 'Now that's where you're wrong, Lizzie.'

'Why? What do you think you've proved?'

'That you do want me.'

Unfortunately, it was true. Lizzie only had to hear Jack say the words—*you want me*—and coils of longing tightened inside her again.

She straightened her shoulders. 'We've been through all the reasons why we can't have a future. Why are you trying to make it hard for me to leave?'

'Because you're being stubborn. You won't admit how you feel.'

She couldn't meet his gaze. If she looked into Jack's eyes again, she'd weaken. 'I have to go, Jack.'

For his sake, she had to be strong. Why couldn't he see he should be with some pretty-eyed, horse-riding country girl? 'This should have been a straightforward holiday romance, and I'm sorry if I let it get out of hand.'

For the longest time Jack didn't speak.

Then Lizzie heard the snap of a twig. Her head jerked up and she saw him toss broken sticks into the water.

The pain in his face made her want to weep.

He wouldn't look at her.

'I have to do this on my own, Jack.' Oh, God. She felt as if she'd volunteered to have surgery without anaesthetic, but she forced the tremors out of her voice. 'I have responsibilities, but they're my responsibilities. Not yours.'

The journey back to Savannah was strained and silent.

'Unless you change your mind, I'd rather you didn't talk,' Jack ordered through tight lips, and he stared straight ahead, knuckles white as he gripped the steering wheel, never once looking Lizzie's way.

The tension was awful—suffocating—and Lizzie sat in an agony of despair. Over and over, she reassured herself that she was doing the right thing. Leaving Savannah was her only option, and she had to make her departure as quick and clean as possible.

It might have been different if she was sure she could make Jack happy, but how could she? He was such an easy-going, and likeable and genuinely warm guy, and if she transplanted him into her world, if he became her life partner, dealing with the pressures of her job, her babies, and her family, he would be forced to change.

How could he be happy then?

Her only solution could be to give up politics, but should she give it up for a man, when she'd stopped trusting men years ago? Where men were concerned she'd totally lost faith in her own judgement, and now, when she'd just had a shock, was the worst possible moment to ditch the wisdom she'd garnered over so many years.

Loving Jack might feel wonderful and right, but with her track record she couldn't trust something as intangible as feelings. Her only sensible option was to stick with her original plan, which meant she had to leave.

Each day she stayed here only messed up Jack's life more, and she cared about him too much to go on hurting him.

By ten o'clock that evening, Lizzie's matching pale green leather suitcases sat, packed and ready, on the floor beside the wardrobe. Her reading material was packed into the green leather holdall, her laptop was stowed away, and she'd organised her charter flight for first thing the next morning.

She had no idea where Jack was. She hadn't seen him at dinner.

Bill told her he'd joined the ringers for a meal and to discuss a problem they had with one of the bores, so she'd eaten alone, and she'd had to leave a note for Jack, explaining her arrangements. Now she was alone again in her room, miserably searching her soul for the five thousandth time.

The problem with soul-searching was that it dug up answers she didn't want to find. Like her feelings for Jack…the way her heart lifted whenever he walked into a room…the way being with him made the simplest things special…the way his skin was warm and smooth beneath her fingers…

She tried to force the thoughts out of her head and to concentrate on the amazing fact that in a little over five months she would have two babies. Two cuddly, snugly, warm and cosy baby boys.

They would be everything Lizzie needed, the perfect, sweet companions. They had to be. Lizzie was pinning her faith on it.

No maternal pressure or anything.

Oh, gosh. Jack had said that on the day she'd arrived at Savannah, when he'd learned that she'd been named after Queen Elizabeth. Now she pressed a hand to her mouth as painful questions clamoured.

Was she asking too much of her little boys? Before the poor darlings had even been born, was she expecting them to fill the Jack-sized gaps in her life?

CHAPTER TWELVE

THE small plane was due to arrive at nine-fifteen.

Jack rose early, skipping breakfast to clear the horses and flatten the anthills on the airstrip. Then he returned to the homestead to find Lizzie's luggage at the bottom of the steps, waiting to be packed into the back of the ute.

He'd been trying to stay numb ever since he'd read her note, and he loaded the suitcases like an automaton. It was the only way he would get through this.

Lizzie had been in the kitchen saying goodbye to Bill, but now she appeared, dressed in Jack's favourite soft blue jeans and the pale green top with the ruffles down the front.

Last week, she'd joked that she wouldn't be able to wear these clothes much longer, and they'd talked about ordering maternity clothes over the Internet. Now she was leaving, and Jack was stunned that it was all happening so fast.

He'd failed. Again.

If he'd been smarter, he would have found a sure-fire way to convince Lizzie that he loved her, that she belonged with him, and he with her. Maybe he should have told her earlier, later, with flowers, on bended knee. Anyway he looked at it, he'd stuffed up.

And Lizzie had morphed back into Senator Green, organising her return to the city and the plane that would fetch her with one efficient touch of a button on her mobile phone.

Now it was too late.

In the skies above Savannah, the plane was already circling like a silver toy, glinting in the sunlight. Even Cobber knew what that meant, and the dog leapt lightly into the back of the ute.

It was time to go.

Apart from a polite hello and a nodded thank-you when Jack opened the door for Lizzie, neither of them could find anything to say on the way to the airstrip. They reached it at the same time the plane landed, amidst its usual cloud of red dust.

Lizzie was pale as she got out of the ute.

Jack had to ask. 'Should you be flying? You don't look well.'

'I'm OK. I didn't sleep much, that's all.' She looked across to the plane. 'Jack, I really do want to thank you for—for everything.'

He was dying inside, but he forced himself to speak. 'Look at me, Lizzie.'

She gave the tiniest shake of her head.

'Lizzie.'

Slowly, she turned, and he saw the sheen of her tears. Her chin trembled.

'I love you,' Jack said, and to his horror his eyes filled with tears, too. 'I love you so much. I'd do anything.'

'Jack, please.' Her tears spilled onto her cheeks. 'Don't make it worse.'

'It can't be any worse.' In despair, he said, 'You know you're going to take a long time to get over this, don't you?'

Her face crumpled, but abruptly she turned and, stumbling a little, she began to walk towards the plane.

Jack didn't follow her. He couldn't bring himself to meekly step forward, carrying her suitcases, when all he wanted to do was to throw her over his shoulder, and stop this insanity.

How could he let her go?

He thought of wild schemes to stop the plane—ripping its propeller out, tearing off its wings.

Already, Lizzie was halfway across the stretch of red dirt that took her to the plane's metal steps.

It was happening. Heaven help him, she was determined to walk out of his life, but it was like watching a loved one die, or walk the green mile. How could she do this to herself?

How would he live without her?

Ahead of him, Lizzie stopped and looked back at him as he stood there with a suitcase in each hand.

She looked at the plane, then to Jack again.

She was clearly hesitating and Jack stood his ground and his heart began to hammer. Blood pounded in his ears.

Only a few more steps.

Eyes wide in a bid to stem the tears, Lizzie stared at the little plane as if, somehow, staring could help. But all she could see was a figure, ridiculously dressed in white, stepping down from that cabin, and seeing Jack for the first time. That had been the beginning...

She looked back at Jack again. He hadn't moved.

Was he going to make her go back to fetch her own bags?

He was standing there, and she knew from the set in his shoulders and the stiff way he held himself that he was hurting. So much.

What am I doing?
Going back to face my responsibilities.
Why?
Good question.

For so long she'd put her career first. Even now, she was turning away from Jack because he wouldn't fit in with her career.

Like someone drowning, Lizzie saw her life at Savannah flash before her—saw the morning she'd worked on the truck's brakes with Jack. Saw herself driving the truck to feed the weaner calves. The over-the-top ossobucco meal. Jack jumping the stockyard gate. Tearing outside to kiss him. Making love. Talking with him long into the night about families.

Families.

Oh, help.

Jack wanted to join her and her boys to create a little family. He loved her. He wanted to love her sons, yet here she was, walking away from him, just as Angelo and Alessandro's mother had walked away from her uncle Luca. Just as her mother had walked from her father…

What-am-I-doing-what-am-I-doing-what-am-I-doing?

How could she do this? To herself? To her boys? Most of all how could she do it to Jack?

How could she pretend that Jack would be happier without her? How many times did he have to tell her that he loved her before she believed him?

As her heart began to break Lizzie turned.

She began to run.

Jack saw Lizzie running.

Tears were streaming down her cheeks, but she was smiling. Laughing.

The bags fell from his hands, tumbling to the ground, and Lizzie, smiling through her tears, ran into his arms.

'I couldn't do it,' she sobbed. 'I love you.'

'Of course you do.'

'I thought I could leave you, but I can't. I couldn't take another step. I was leaving for all the wrong reasons. I wanted you to be happy, but it's not going to work, is it? If I leave we'll both be unhappy for the rest of our lives.'

'Darling girl.'

'This is not a plea for help with the babies, Jack.' She touched her fingers to his lips. 'This is just about you, and how I feel about you.'

He kissed her fingers, her nose, her eyelids.

'We can make it work. I can leave politics.'

'Not on my account, Senator. Only if you want to.'

'I've done enough. I want to leave. I want you, Jack. I want us to be a family. I promise I'll make you happy.'

'You've already made me happy.' He would have swung her around and around, if he weren't worried about making her dizzy. Instead, he kissed her again, on the chin, on the ear, then said, 'There's only one thing that could make me any happier.'

'I'll do anything. I love you. What is it?'

'Marry me.'

A sudden voice called from behind them, 'Is everything all right, Senator Green?'

The pilot, clearly puzzled, had climbed down from the cockpit.

'Everything's fine,' Lizzie called back to him. 'Jack's asked me to marry him and I'm about to give him my answer.'

Turning her back on the plane, she looked joyously

into Jack's eyes. 'And the answer's yes. A thousand times yes. I promise we're going to have the happiest marriage of all time.'

Although the Italian summer was just around the corner, it was cool on Sorella's terrace when Lizzie took Jack outside to show him her favourite Monta Correnti view.

'Come here,' he said, noticing that she'd shivered, and putting his arms around her. 'Let me keep you warm.'

Lizzie laughed. 'Any time.'

Snuggling against him, she looked out over the sea of pale terracotta rooftops to the sloping green rows of the vineyards and the neat olive groves, and further on across the valley to the distant purple hills. 'What do you think of my home town?'

'Amazing. It's so beautiful here. I don't know how you ever left.'

'Beautiful landscapes can only go so far,' she said. 'They can't actually make you happy.'

Jack kissed her cheek. 'I won't argue with that.'

Turning in his arms, Lizzie smiled at him and held out her left hand to admire, yet again, her beautiful green sapphire engagement ring. 'These last few days have been the happiest days of my life.'

'And the busiest.'

'Yes.' She remembered all the meetings, the press conferences…especially the one with Jack at her side helping to explain about her pregnancy and her choices for the future. It was all behind them now. 'I'm so glad I've resigned. Such bliss. I still haven't got used to the freedom.'

'I don't think you'll regret it.'

'I won't, Jack. I know I won't. I promise. I just love

knowing that we're both free to make whatever plans we want for our marriage, and our own little family.'

She was rewarded by a warm hug and another kiss, on the lips this time.

When they drew apart, she said, 'What do you think of my mother's offer to hold our wedding reception in Romano's palazzo?'

'It's a very generous offer.'

'She's trying to make up for all the trouble she's caused.'

'A palazzo sounds very grand.'

'It is rather grand.'

'Would you like a reception there?'

'I have to admit it's a fairy-tale setting. On Lake Adrina.' Lizzie slipped her arms around Jack. 'Don't be alarmed, but I'm thinking it would be wonderful if we had a really big wedding and invited everyone in the family—even my long-lost cousins from New York.'

Jack grinned. 'I'll go along with anything as long as we tie the knot.'

'And I'll invite my sisters, of course.' Lizzie was pensive for a moment. 'There's been a silly problem between Scarlett and my cousin Isabella ever since they were children. Actually, Scarlett doesn't get on too well with Jackie either, for that matter. Our wedding can be the perfect excuse to bring the family back together.'

'Then there's no question,' Jack said. 'Let's invite the lot.'

'I'll ring everyone tonight to warn them to start making plans.' With a tender smile, Lizzie traced the line of his jaw. 'Have you noticed, my darling, that you've been a huge hit with every member of my family that you've met so far?'

'They've been very kind to me.'

'Kind?' Lizzie laughed. 'They're smitten. They adore you,

Jack. You've charmed them to pieces. Especially my mother. Even Isabella, and she's madly in love with her Max.'

Isabella, however, wasn't quite so charmed when Lizzie rang her later that evening to tell her the latest wedding plans.

'Romano's palazzo?' Isabella was clearly agitated. 'Why would you want a reception there?'

'Why not? It's a gorgeous setting on Lake Adrina. I thought it would be perfect.'

'Yes, it's beautiful, but—'

'But *what*, Isabella?' It was hard not to sound annoyed. 'You're as bad as Scarlett.'

There was a distinct gasp on the other end of the line. 'Have you been talking to Scarlett?'

'Of course. She's my sister, after all.'

'Well, yes.' Isabella's voice was thin and decidedly anxious. 'What did Scarlett say when you told her about the palazzo?'

'Her reaction was almost the same as yours. She wasn't happy, but when I pressed her she couldn't give me any proper reason. It didn't make sense.'

'I suppose it is silly to be worked up about a venue.' Isabella sounded distinctly calmer now.

'It is if neither of you can give me a solid reason why I shouldn't have the reception there.'

Later, in bed in the best guest room in Lisa's villa, complete with marble floors and views through arched windows to the diamond-studded sky, Lizzie confided in Jack. 'I'm beginning to think this wedding of ours will either make or break my family.'

'You worry too much. It'll work out fine.'

'How can you be sure?'

He nuzzled her neck, drawing her in. 'We're so in love it's going to rub off on the others.'

Lizzie wrapped her arms around him. 'Wouldn't it be wonderful if you were right?'

'I am.' Jack's lips met hers, the first kiss of the night. 'You wait and see.'

* * * * *

Harlequin offers a romance for every mood!
See below for a sneak peek from our suspense romance line
Silhouette® Romantic Suspense.
Introducing HER HERO IN HIDING by
New York Times *bestselling author Rachel Lee.*

Kay Young returned to woozy consciousness to find that she was lying on a soft sofa beneath a heap of quilts near a cheerfully burning fire. When she tried to move, however, everything hurt, and she groaned.

At once she heard a sound, then a stranger with a hard, harsh face was squatting beside her. "Shh," he said softly. "You're safe here. I promise."

"I have to go," she said weakly, struggling against pain. "He'll find me. He can't find me."

"Easy, lady," he said quietly. "You're hurt. No one's going to find you here."

"He will," she said desperately, terror clutching at her insides. "He always finds me!"

"Easy," he said again. "There's a blizzard outside. No one's getting here tonight, not even the doctor. I know, because I tried."

"Doctor? I don't need a doctor! I've got to get away."

"There's nowhere to go tonight," he said levelly. "And if I thought you could stand, I'd take you to a window and show you."

But even as she tried once more to pull away the quilts, she remembered something else: this man had been gentle when he'd found her beside the road, even when she had kicked and clawed. He hadn't hurt her.

Terror receded just a bit. She looked at him and detected signs of true concern there.

The terror eased another notch and she let her head sag on the pillow. "He always finds me," she whispered.

"Not here. Not tonight. That much I can guarantee."

*Will Kay's mysterious rescuer protect her
from her worst fears?
Find out in HER HERO IN HIDING
by New York Times bestselling author Rachel Lee.
Available June 2010,
only from Silhouette® Romantic Suspense.*

HARLEQUIN® *Romance*®

GIRLS'
Weekend in
VEGAS

Four friends, four dream weddings!

On a girly weekend in Las Vegas, best friends Alex, Molly,
Serena and Jayne are supposed to just have fun and forget
men, but they end up meeting their perfect matches!
Will the love they find in Vegas stay in Vegas?

Find out in this sassy, fun and wildly romantic miniseries
all about love and friendship!

═══════════════════

Saving Cinderella! by MYRNA MACKENZIE
Available June

Vegas Pregnancy Surprise by SHIRLEY JUMP
Available July

Inconveniently Wed! by JACKIE BRAUN
Available August

Wedding Date with the Best Man
by MELISSA MCCLONE
Available September

www.eHarlequin.com

HRI7663

LARGER-PRINT BOOKS!

GET 2 FREE LARGER-PRINT NOVELS PLUS
2 FREE GIFTS!

HARLEQUIN® *Romance*®

From the Heart, For the Heart

YES! Please send me 2 FREE LARGER-PRINT Harlequin® Romance novels and my 2 FREE gifts (gifts are worth about $10). After receiving them, if I don't wish to receive any more books, I can return the shipping statement marked "cancel." If I don't cancel, I will receive 6 brand-new novels every month and be billed just $4.07 per book in the U.S. or $4.47 per book in Canada. That's a saving of at least 22% off the cover price! It's quite a bargain! Shipping and handling is just 50¢ per book.* I understand that accepting the 2 free books and gifts places me under no obligation to buy anything. I can always return a shipment and cancel at any time. Even if I never buy another book from Harlequin, the two free books and gifts are mine to keep forever.

186/386 HDN E5N4

Name _____ (PLEASE PRINT)

Address _____ Apt. #

City _____ State/Prov. _____ Zip/Postal Code

Signature (if under 18, a parent or guardian must sign)

Mail to the **Harlequin Reader Service:**
IN U.S.A.: P.O. Box 1867, Buffalo, NY 14240-1867
IN CANADA: P.O. Box 609, Fort Erie, Ontario L2A 5X3

Not valid for current subscribers to Harlequin Romance Larger-Print books.

Are you a current subscriber to Harlequin Romance books and want to receive the larger-print edition? Call 1-800-873-8635 today!

* Terms and prices subject to change without notice. Prices do not include applicable taxes. N.Y. residents add applicable sales tax. Canadian residents will be charged applicable provincial taxes and GST. Offer not valid in Quebec. This offer is limited to one order per household. All orders subject to approval. Credit or debit balances in a customer's account(s) may be offset by any other outstanding balance owed by or to the customer. Please allow 4 to 6 weeks for delivery. Offer available while quantities last.

Your Privacy: Harlequin Books is committed to protecting your privacy. Our Privacy Policy is available online at www.eHarlequin.com or upon request from the Reader Service. From time to time we make our lists of customers available to reputable third parties who may have a product or service of interest to you. ☐ If you would prefer we not share your name and address, please check here.

Help us get it right—We strive for accurate, respectful and relevant communications. To clarify or modify your communication preferences, visit us at www.ReaderService.com/consumerschoice.

HRLP10R

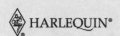

HARLEQUIN®

Showcase

On sale May 11, 2010

Reader favorites from the most talented voices in romance

Save $1.00 on the purchase of 1 or more Harlequin® Showcase books.

SAVE $1.00 on the purchase of 1 or more Harlequin® Showcase books.

Coupon expires Oct 31, 2010. Redeemable at participating retail outlets.
Limit one coupon per purchase. Valid in the U.S.A. and Canada only.

52609015

Canadian Retailers: Harlequin Enterprises Limited will pay the face value of this coupon plus 10.25¢ if submitted by customer for this product only. Any other use constitutes fraud. Coupon is nonassignable. Void if taxed, prohibited or restricted by law. Consumer must pay any government taxes. Void if copied. Nielsen Clearing House ("NCH") customers submit coupons and proof of sales to Harlequin Enterprises Limited, P.O. Box 3000, Saint John, NB E2L 4L3, Canada. Non-NCH retailer—for reimbursement submit coupons and proof of sales directly to Harlequin Enterprises Limited, Retail Marketing Department, 225 Duncan Mill Rd., Don Mills, ON M3B 3K9, Canada.

5 65373 00076 2 (8100)0 11651

U.S. Retailers: Harlequin Enterprises Limited will pay the face value of this coupon plus 8¢ if submitted by customer for this product only. Any other use constitutes fraud. Coupon is nonassignable. Void if taxed, prohibited or restricted by law. Consumer must pay any government taxes. Void if copied. For reimbursement submit coupons and proof of sales directly to Harlequin Enterprises Limited, P.O. Box 880478, El Paso, TX 88588-0478, U.S.A. Cash value 1/100 cents.

HSCCOUP0410

Coming Next Month

Available June 8, 2010

#4171 THE LIONHEARTED COWBOY RETURNS
Patricia Thayer
The Texas Brotherhood

#4172 MIRACLE FOR THE GIRL NEXT DOOR
Rebecca Winters
The Brides of Bella Rosa

#4173 THREE TIMES A BRIDESMAID...
Nicola Marsh
In Her Shoes...

#4174 THEIR NEWBORN GIFT
Nikki Logan
Outback Baby Tales

#4175 SAVING CINDERELLA!
Myrna Mackenzie
Girls' Weekend in Vegas

#4176 A DINNER, A DATE, A DESERT SHEIKH
Jackie Braun
Desert Brides

HRCNMBPA0510R